SPIDER BOYS

SPIDER
BOYS

MING CHER

WILLIAM MORROW
AND COMPANY, INC.
NEW YORK

It is the policy of William Morrow and Company, Inc., and its imprints and affiliates,
recognizing the importance of preserving what has been written, to print the books
we publish on acid-free paper, and we exert our best efforts to that end.

Library of Congress Cataloging-in-Publication Data

Cher, Ming.
Spider boys / Ming Cher.
p.   cm.
ISBN 0-688-12858-0
I. Title.
PS3553.H352S65   1995
813'.54—dc20   94-38310
CIP

Printed in the United States of America

First Edition

1 2 3 4 5 6 7 8 9 10

BOOK DESIGN BY BRIAN MULLIGAN

This novel is dedicated to my parents, and especially

to my son, Marco Ming Cher.

A number of people have helped me with this novel. I would like to thank Bronwyn Sprague and Craig Miller, and especially my agents, Michael Gifkins and Sandra Dijkstra, who made it all possible.

Contents

List of Characters

Kwang (also known as Shark Head and Monkey Boy)—son of Pau Shen (deceased) and Yee; leader of spider boys

Kim (Swee Kim)—daughter of Ah Hock

Ah Seow (real name Tain Seng)—Kwang's deputy; brother of Kim

Yee—Kwang's mother

Pau Shen (the Kung Fu man)—Kwang's father (deceased)

Ah Hock—Kim's father

Chai—son of Big Head; Kwang's spider rival

Chinatown Yeow (also known as Smiling Boy)—leader of Chinatown boys

San—Chai's deputy; son of Wong

No Nose—village kite-maker

Blind Man—village storyteller

Wong—village calligrapher; father of San

Big Head—gambling den operator; father of Chai

Ah Paw—Chai's grandmother

Big Mole—orphaned Chinatown girl; protector of Sachee

Sachee—orphaned Chinatown boy; spy for Yeow

Ah Sow (also known as Cigarette Woman)—Yeow's adoptive mother (godmother)

Cheong Pak—husband of Ah Sow; Yeow's adoptive father (godfather)

Ng Koo—rich widow; high-class brothel owner

Shoot Bird—merchant; initiator of Spider Olympic Games

Hong—burglar; former spider boy

SPIDER BOYS

SINGAPORE

1 9 5 5

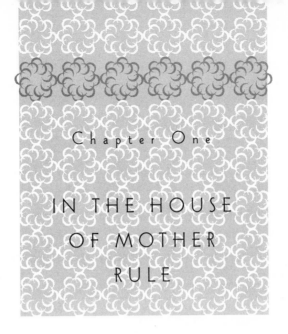

IN THE HOUSE
OF MOTHER
RULE

The unique wrestling spider
is a nomadic hunter living in between sandwich
leaves, black in color and fully tattooed with
shining spots and stripes, either in dark green,
turquoise, blue, red, or even purple, which
makes it psychedelic. Body is shape and size like
a grain of rice, head is half a rice and broader.
Female has black face, male has white face and
slimmer body, longer legs and forearms with a
needly penis at its end which gives it a scorpion
image. Is a jealous sex maniac who can't resist
the sight of a female. Mad at fellow males and

war dance before they fight. Jumps quick like a Ping-Pong ball when caught fresh. Spider boys all over Singapore, catch them for petting, betting, and selling, call them Panther Tiger. Kwang was hypnotize by it ever since he learn to walk and talk.

Kwang and Kim grow up like sweethearts in the house with the bamboo deck their fathers built together. Ah Hock's daughter, Kim, like to watch him blew wind at the female to sit still, and thumbs the bum gently on a flat tin box supported by four fingers underneath. Then let out a male from another box to hop in. At the sight of her, the sex-hungry male will raise its arm in a frenzy to seek entry under Kwang's thumb, which make the female wriggles about, like pleading, "Help me . . . ! Help me . . . !" to the desperate male under the blinking eyes of Kwang and Kim watching the actions.

"Hey," she point at the male. "Can you see the needle on the spider tail get longer now. . . . You know why?"

"Of course . . . !" he eye at her. "That one is the male, white face. The needle is like my thing, here . . . !" And pull down his elastic shorts to flips his prick up and down until it grow. "Same like mine, a male can expand . . . !"

Kim touch his thing and giggles. He jerk with a shiver.

Sometimes they pretend to be spiders and wrestling together. Sometimes he ride on her like a male spider. Until his strict mother found out and give him his first big whacking for cocking Kim just before he turn seven years old. Yee told Ah Hock's wife. Kim was also cane. Ah Hock, a tall strong coolie, was furious at the cane mark on her body and nearly beat up his wife who love her son, Tain Seng, more. From then on Kim was free to do what she like.

Even after his father, Pau Shen the Kung Fu man, died when he was ten years old, Kwang's love for wrestling spider never die. When his mother, who hates spider, is at home he will pretend to study hard, reading any English word that comes to his mind. "A—boy, C—dog . . . ! B—orange." Anyhow before a book to bullshit his mother who can't read and write in any language. For she will look please to leave him alone.

Kim's year-younger brother, Tain Seng, is nickname Ah Seow (Something Wrong) by all the spider boys in the village, for fits of psychic hallucinations when he gets very nervous. Otherwise is brilliant at school and good at spider business.

Ah Seow is Kwang's spider agent and safeguard against fierce Yee knowing about it.

Kwang goes to school in the morning session and Ah Seow in the afternoon. When Kim was twelve years old, her mother went to work as a live-in servant, coming home twice a month. Kim runs the housekeeping. Their mothers had big quarrels. But for them business is as usual.

One night, through the gaps of rough plank walls dividing their bedrooms, Kwang whisper, "Ah Seow, Ah Seow . . . keep this one for me." And pass him a spider box.

"Only one?" Ah Seow took it and report, "There are only two of your other spider left, the rest all sold."

"Don't talk so loud and so much, lah . . . !" Kwang growl quietly. "My mother is in a bad mood. I wait for you in the usual place before cock crows. Can you wake up earlier?" Inside mosquito net on raise up plank floor which is the bed he shares with his two younger brothers.

"You climb over and wake me up, lah," said Ah Seow in his usual submissive voice when Kwang demands something from him. He rely on Kwang for protection against other village bullies since growing up.

The next morning they crawl out of their mosquito nets and jump out of the bedroom window into the narrow alley between neighbor's wall at the back of their house.

Ah Seow clap away the dust from the jump and moan. "So early . . . !" Rubbing his long sleepy eyes on the sleeves of his shirt, spider boxes inside a canvas bag over his shoulder.

"Don't talk prick words!" Kwang elbow at him lightly. "I tell you something when we get there, run!" He push him for a race. They cut corners and up slopes, passing the backyard of a farmhouse on to a small plot of big yam leaves which pools morning dew on its waxy surface.

Ah Seow ask breathlessly, "What is the big news?"

Kwang ignore him and turn to tilt a big yam leaf, to and fro to watch dewdrops merging with smaller drops on the waxy surface, dreamily in his own world for a while. "Bring out the spiders," he order. "Bring out the Panther Tigers. . . ." Scratching his lean shirtless body scarred by mosquito bites from catching spiders and unhealed cane marks from his mother who want him to stay at home and study hard.

Ah Seow squats down to take out two metal cigarette case from his canvas bag. "Sold at six for one-dollar-fifty, only the best two is left," he report and pass him a box.

"Not this one . . . ! The one from last night." Kwang tighten his lips bossily at his assistant.

Ah Seow knew him inside out, knew he was in a boastful mood. "Oh . . . !" he slap his forehead. "I forget to bring that box!" To poke him around.

"Real or not . . . ?" Kwang frown from his thick brows at Seow with his odd look. His mother crops his thick black hair flat two inches above his ears, like he was capped by half a coconut shell to save the barber's money on his bulging forehead. So much so, when water is pour on top of his head, he could see the water falling like waterfalls cascading before his eyes and maintain his quite flat nose dry on his tight face and small mean eyes.

Ah Seow, a tallish handsome boy, give up, smiling broadly, and took the wanted box which he hides at the back of his elastic shorts under the shirt. "Na . . . !" He hand it over.

"Don't talk prick words and waste time, lah!" Kwang snatch the box and ask with a proud new face, "Have you seen it?"

Ah Seow jerk his shoulder with open palm and fire back, "Dare not see, wait for you . . . !"

Kwang open the spider box which has two box-sized Pandan leaves fitted inside upon each other and tap, taps with a finger on the top leaf which has a hole in the center for a Mr. Wrestling Spider to come out. The white-face male spider crawl out from the hole like yawning, with its arms lifting up and down, ready to adjust itself to the outside world of morning just after cock crows, looking ready to jump and relax its muscles.

"Come on, jump, jump." Kwang urges his spider with his brows up and down quietly. And it doesn't take long for his Mr. Spider to respond and jump into his palm, his other hand move in front to con it to jump again, jumping between two hands, creating longer and longer distance, measuring how far his new pet can jump in the longest leap below his nose and shifting eyes capturing its movements. After a few minutes session, he let the thirsty creature jump into a big leaf to walk about and drink morning dew. Watching his new pet all the way seems to carry him in another world that still puzzles Ah Seow.

As he observes, he snaps his fingers 'and palm out a hand. "Ah Seow . . . Ah Seow, pass me my bedbugs."

Ah Seow land a small Tiger Balm tin case on his palm and stoop closer. "Rare purple!" he comment. "Try it out yet?"

"No need to, lah . . . !" Kwang said confidently. "Block the spider in your palm and see how heavy it bounce."

While Ah Seow feels the new spider jumping between hands, Kwang nips out the fattest bedbug alive from the Tiger Balm case which feed from his own blood, caught beneath the straw mats on his bed. "Heavy?" he ask. "I feed it first." Scooping the spider swiftly on the box toward his breast, he blow at it to sit still, and drop the bedbug on the box surface for the spider to pounce at his meal the moment he stop blowing.

Breakfast on the mouth, spider look up like a tiny friend in real life talking below the nose of a giant friend. "I want a dark place to enjoy my meal." He guide his fresh pet into the box, snaps the lid. And beam at Ah Seow. "The snappy bites on the bug's neck is so fast and accurate. See something about the head?"

Ah Seow begins to see. "Ya, ya," he nods. "The head is much broader than usual, where you catch it?"

"At the end of Number Ten STC bus terminal behind the row of hawker stalls in the large pit of rubbish dumps," said Kwang. Biggering his small and mean piercing black eyes that has anger, scared from crying within, crying freedom, "Freedom from mother's rule!"

Ah Seow stand back and said, "But that place . . . that place was burnt by a big fire two years ago?"

"It is green again . . . ! Different leaves, too. Pandan and lalang now cover up the whole place with a lot of mosquitoes and flying red fleas breed from the wet rubbish dump by the hawkers." Talking faster as he scratches his shirtless scar body. "They like the red fleas, that is why their colors is so dark purple."

Ah Seow's brains wake up. "There must be a lot more!"

"I spend nearly an hour, then I caught this one, another one escape . . . ! Remember? Remember the Blind Man always say in his stories? After a fire, if anything live again, it is very strong. I can tell by the look of this Panther Tiger."

Ah Seow ask quickly, "Do you want to match against Chai?"

"This time I will win back all the money I lost to Chai," the boss proclaim with the yellow spider box in his hand and squats down. "Ah Seow, how much money all together?"

Ah Seow squats in front of him and took out two spider boxes and money from his bag. "Na," he said. "One dollar sixty—if I sell this two best ones at forty cents each, all together two-forty. Na, one-sixty." Throwing the coins on the ground naked of vegetation caused by their attendance regularly.

The boss stoops to pocket the money and throw back twenty cents on the ground. "Na . . . ! Your commission." With a bare foot pushing the two spider boxes toward Ah Seow. "Sell it for me, I need the capital to go back and catch more before anybody found out the new place. Feed the old spiders with fly heads, save the other bedbugs for my new spider to eat."

Ah Seow collects all the boxes into his bag and rubs his twenty-cent coin on the hand. "How much do you think Chai have?"

"What about you, how much can you lend me?"

"One dollar the most," said Ah Seow with head thinking groundward.

"Not enough . . . ! I need three dollars!" Kwang explode. "I want to skip school for a few more days to catch more."

"Why don't you ask my sister? She has all the marketing money from Mama and Papa."

"Cannot! I already owe her five dollars, Kim is not talking to me anymore. If you don't trust me just say so . . . !"

"The most is two dollars," Ah Seow make his offer firmly. "No more . . . !"

The boss walk and said, "I want the money today."

More cocks crows in the early morning. Walking, talking down from farming area. Ah Seow advise, "The place is so far away, bus fares, eating outside in that expensive area will cost you at least eighty cents a day even if you don't use Tiger Balm to stop mosquito bites. Remember? The last time, you win, win until Chai nearly lost his temper and nearly start a fight with you again, the next day we lost everything in that big match . . . ?"

The boss punch his palm. "We lost in the sixth round!" Think again and punch harder. "Get caught by my mother the next day too. That time my luck was really bad. Fucking mother's cunt!" He swear and look at some hard-to-heal old cane marks.

"Everybody is still talking about it at the banyan tree."

"This time, this time is going to be different." He shoot a glance at Ah Seow and start counting his finger. "This Saturday and Sunday my mother is working on night shift, I cannot come out . . . have to wait for maybe something like ten days."

Ah Seow remind him as they plot along. "I can guarantee everybody will save up for a return match between you and Chai, but what about our capitals?"

"I see what I can catch first, if good, I will try it out with the Chinatown shoeshine boys first, make capital first."

"You mean those street boys?" Ah Seow warn, "Don't touch them, too risky! They use knives, can't fight with them, they throw red pepper on your face in a group, not gentlemen . . . !"

"I know . . . I am not that stupid, I meet their chief."

"You mean Chinatown Yeow? That king of street boy . . . !"

"Ya, lah!" He air with a bit of modesty. "I talk to him about me in his territory over a cup of coffee. He agree everybody should be gentleman when win or lose."

Ah Seow who hero-worship tough boy get excited. "How do you meet him? What do you think of him?" Curiously on Yeow who is legendary even among the adult gangs in Chinatown.

"When we do well, I introduce him to you," he jab on his assistant's arm with a tilt of his head. "Let's run . . . !"

After climbing back into his bedroom, it didn't take long to hear him shouting, "Wake up! Wake up!" At his four and five years younger brothers for a wash in the well. "One! Two! Three!" he shout and throw the bucket in the well. "One! Two! Three!" his brothers sing, he pull the bucket out of the well. Using empty cans, they scoop up water, throwing at each other, laughing, giggling merrily. Running home after each other, eating anything that is available for breakfast while the mother is still sleeping from a late shift laboring job on ship. Food is usually plain rice with soy sauce, more than that is a feast. He has say many times to

Kim and Ah Seow, "If my mother treat me like Chai's father, no need to go to school. I can make more money than my mother." He has secretly supply extra food for his kid brothers from spider money. An average spider can fetch up to twenty cents, can buy two bowls of rich curry laksa soup, very delicious to go with plain rice, or two salted eggs, or three fresh.

Chapter Two

SPIDER MATCHING

Kwang skip school and went back to STC bus terminal on a low-budget trip without using Tiger Balm against mosquito bites. After a few hours he caught two spiders. "Fucking prick mosquitoes!" he curse and scratches all the way out of the bushy big pit of rubbish dumps to cross the road. And sit on the bench of an Indian cart stall by the roadside under a tree. "Teh . . . !" He raise a finger for tea in Malay at the burly Indian sitting behind two 20-gallon copper drums of hot water boiling over slow charcoal fire. And help himself to his favorite curry bun inside a glass jar on the counter.

Kwang gobbles down two buns quickly. And peep at his new catch jumping madly inside a flat metal box, bedded with leaves, trying to escape out of the box, all the time! He kept blowing wind at it to calm it down and sit still for a quick look. And snap the lid quickly to prevent the jumpy spider getting executed on the edges when the lid shut.

"Teh . . . !" said the big Indian with voice deep like drum. And pass the glass of cardamom tea through the space between the two copper drums.

After a few quick sips at the hot tea, Kwang point at the wrist. "Baaboo?" To ask the time at the Indian with a nickname for being big and hairy in Malay. Baaboo wince at being call big and hairy. But he still stretch over his wrist on his hairy hand between the drums for him to look at the time. Kwang thanks Baaboo with a quick salute, hands his glass of tea back to him with his tongue rolling in and out to say it is too hot.

Baaboo has long mustache neatly curved up. "Aachaa [Cheeky]!" he growl as he took Kwang's glass and sit down to cool the hot tea, pouring it between two glasses with expert hand.

Kwang took the opportunity to take off like a whip to catch the 11:15 bus heading for Chinatown. Without paying for his bread.

At Chinatown, he went straight to Nam Tain Lane which is a night market, quiet in the afternoon. He is a stranger inside this territory. About a few dozen street kids from seven to fifteen years old occupy the dead end of Nam Tain Lane, gambling against each other all the time. Squatting in patches, some play Ting Tong with two coins, matchsticks guessing, cards, and matching wrestling spiders. Kwang could feel the vibes of walking in a jungle, watched by all kinds of animal faces. But want to make money through spider matching with these cash-rich Chinatown boys. At a short distance away, he take a deep breath to steady his nerve with a hand gripping the strap of his schoolbag before entering the den of those impulsive gambling street kids.

One of them who sit on a shoeshine box yell out, "Shark Head!" with a random nickname for his odd look. "Shark Head!" he yell again. "Come over here . . . !" Waving his finger backward slowly to ridicule him like a dog.

Kwang walk toward him and force out a smile. "Have you seen Chinatown Yeow?" Mentioning their leader's name like a passport.

The boy in his early youth with short spiky hair scan at him from head to toe with goldfish eyes. "Find Chinatown Yeow for what business?" he ask and thumb at himself. "Talk to me first!"

Watch by all those animal eyes, Kwang felt it was a test of raw guts. "Not your business," he warn Goldfish with a finger. "I came to look for Yeow. Don't disgrace me like a dog with your finger. . . . Okay?" And turn around to face the animal eyes. "Anybody want to have a clash with my Panther Tiger?" Imitating spiders wrestling with two hands.

Sitting behind Kwang's back on his shoeshine box, Goldfish don't want to lose face, he lurch forward to grab at the strap of Kwang's schoolbag and pull. Kwang slip the strap down from his shoulder with a Kung Fu "excreting stand" to firm himself and pull back. Goldfish pull harder, Kwang frees the belt, Goldfish bums backward and stood up quickly, Kwang lifts a knee to strike at his balls the moment he stood up.

"Aayaak . . . !" Goldfish scream and bend down with face turn white instantly.

Kwang tips his eyes left and right at those animal eyes and warn Goldfish with a finger. "Don't try and big eat small around . . . I am not good to eat."

Squatting Goldfish can't bear his honor written off with his mates watching. The moment the pain subsides, Goldfish jumps at Kwang with a straight punch. Kwang twist his waist for it to fly past, and chop at the back of Goldfish elbow in a lightning move taught by his Kung Fu father since walking age. Goldfish holds his right elbow with shivering pains.

The fight was over in seconds. Kwang said, "If I don't give face to Yeow, I already break your hand." With folded arms.

Kwang knew he can't run away in a tigers' den if they all mob-attack him, knew that they will attack like a pack of wolves if any one of them is leader enough to order "Saak! [Kill!]." They crowd around with skeptic looks and didn't break away for him to pass.

He introduce himself. "I am from Ho Swee Hill, I came here to play spiders."

Those boys were leaderless for a reply, they start to loosen up and look at each other.

Then he bluff, "Where is Chinatown Yeow? I can't find him in Sentang." To bring up their boss name for second thoughts before they grew wild. And walk out.

Outside the mouth of Nam Tain Lane he start to run for a mile to catch up with the lost time to Pearl Bank School, to join scatter crowds of schoolboys who play spiders before the school bell rings for the afternoon session at 1:15. He ask a familiar face, "Win or lose?"

"Lost four match."

"Lost where?"

"There . . . !" Familiar Face point to a crowd of school kids.

"Use mine to make some eats. . . . Want or not?"

"How? They all scare to bite with you."

"Just don't let them know."

"No money already."

"Money on me, make a bit yourself. Loss not your problem."

"How much you want to throw down?"

Kwang count out his coins to the last cent and win a few dollars from Pearl Bank School. Then he rush to Pearl Hill School to catch up with Ah Seow, who begins his afternoon class at 1:30, to keep his spiders and play safe just in case his mother get suspicious and search him.

When he arrive home, he lie. "Mama, my teacher chose me to be a school prefect. Have to go for meeting tomorrow. Tomorrow I come home late."

The next day he sneak around to avoid Baaboo's stall. Eat inside a coffee shop. With Tiger Balm to stop mosquito bites, he caught five more spiders at the same place. Went to Chinatown Yeow and complain. "Yeow, I mention your name. Your boys in Nam Tain Lane still don't give face. . . . What happen to what you say?"

"You don't fight them, you don't know them," Chinatown Yeow smile. "I have just pass the word around. Check it out yourself." And walk away.

Early next morning. On their way to exercise spiders at their regular place, Kwang pull Ah Seow backward by the collar. "Walk slowly," he said and flash out a red crispy ten-dollar note around the nose with a twinkle little smile.

"Waah . . . !" Ah Seow exclaim. "How many matches altogether?"

"Didn't count, win everywhere. Somebody offer me one dollar for this one." He toss a round spider box in the air to catch it with a leap. "Let's run . . . !"

On arrival at their usual place, he pull out a magnifying glass. "Do you know what this is for?"

"To look at the spider," Ah Seow reply. "What is there to show off?" But he was surprise. He has never seen anybody using a magnifying glass to study spider. He poke about. "What for? Where do you copycat?"

"Don't disgrace me. . . . I don't copycat anybody else," Kwang snap back and trace his spider's movement on the big yam leaves.

Ah Seow knew he can never see what his boss sees in spider, but he knew Kwang will never stop dreaming to win the grand prize in the annual wrestling spider championship among the best of hard-core spider boys through the fifty-two districts of Singapore.

After studying his spiders one by one with his magnifying glass, from feeding to the way they drink morning dew on the big yam leaves, he pick the best two and push the rest toward Ah Seow. "Na . . . ! Fight five matches with Chai at one dollar a match tomorrow, win or lose never mind, but remember the spiders and the rounds in every match."

"What is the new tricks?" Ah Seow ask and pack the spider boxes in the bag.

"You wait and see," Kwang said slowly. "I must go back to school and pay my school fees, if I get the sack from school my mother will finish me." Mumbling with a worried face in a changing mood as they walk.

"How many days have you skip school?"

"Three days straight . . . hard to explain to my pig-face teacher this time."

"If I am you, I will say my parent got no money to pay school fees. They ask me to stay at home. . . ."

"Done that before!" he erupt. "That fucking-face teacher make me stand behind the classroom, for half a day! I have to see the school principal if it happens again."

Knowing his pride, Ah Seow poke about. "Will your legs be shaking if you face the school principal?"

"Don't prick talk, lah . . . !" He jab a playful punch on Seow's arm. Fully aware that the same old lies has to be repeat again. By nature he is a quiet person, a dreamer with inscrutable schemes and tricks privately. Ah Seow, a sensitive boy, follows him like his alter ego.

Walking their way home in the fresh morning before the village awakes. Printing their naked footprints on the muddy tracks. Ah Seow has a fair idea about him using the five spiders to test Chai's spiders. Exactly how is his boss going to plan his next move? Ah Seow is not sure, he fish around. "What have you seen in your glass?"

"You don't know anything about Panther Tiger," the boss scorn as they walk. Walking without a word for a while and then said dreamily, "I want to know everything about Panther Tiger. Sometimes I like to be a Panther Tiger. . . . What my mother hates is what I like . . . !" All of a sudden.

"What did you see?"

"Ask Swee Kim."

"My sister? I thought she didn't like Panther Tiger anymore since our mother big quarrels. She blames you. What she said?"

"She say it has a crab face, I said it has a monkey face and let her look with my magnifying glass closely."

"And then?"

"And then Kim say I have a monkey face like spider. I jump at her, she keep laughing nonstop," he said with a cheeky glance at Ah Seow and take off down the slope.

Ah Seow shouts after him, "You disturb my sister again!" Although a few months younger, Kim has just suddenly shoot up to more than half a head taller than Kwang. Her usual skirt turn into miniskirt, her light cotton T-shirt pops out the vibrant buds of breast flowering at puberty age. Kwang like to rubs on her forming bottom and say, "Big bum!" Grinningly. And she always bark back, "Snake head mouse eyes!" In mock anger with her always ready to laugh eyes at his odd look.

The next day, Saturday, Kwang's mother was at home with housework. He pretend to study hard like usual, reciting any English word that crosses his mind to bullshit her.

In a low-key match with Chai's deputy, San, the son of Wong, at the playground shaded by the huge banyan tree in the afternoon, their spiders won three matches out of five watched by only a few dozen spider boys betting.

When Ah Seow came back with the news, he heard Yee's loud warning noises. "You look after your brothers, if I come home and hear complaints about you . . . ! I will give you a big meal [whacking]!" And turn to Kwang's two little brothers. "Same for the two of you! Remember what I say . . . behave yourself! I will take you all out to eat Cha Sui Pow once a month if you all behave yourself."

The youngest son ask, "How many can I eat?"

Hard work and strains has made Yee look ten years older than her age, has choking anger in her staunch eyes that frightens Kwang like hell. She melts down a little, digs into her pocket to give the youngest ten cents. And raise her voice at Kwang. "You listen carefully! I am leaving you to look after the house. I have found a good permanent job as a second cook in a very rich man's house. The rice drum is full enough for a month." And took out her money to count it twice, with thoughts of her hard life, with hope at Kwang whom she thinks is a star at school, because he bluff her with false school reports.

In a way, she was pleased, sniff up her tears and hand him the money. "There is forty dollars here, one dollar a day for food at home, twenty cents a day for schooling. Come and see me once a week. I want to know what happen at home. This rich people has a son same age as you, make friend with him. . . . That will help to keep the rice bowl going. . . . Have to be smarter than other people nowadays."

"I know, I know," Kwang nods tactfully.

"Clean yourself up. Then I show you my boss place."

Kwang hurry himself with a towel over his shoulder to the common well, with a brand-new face, with heart and mind singing. "Freedom! Freedom to be free and wild at last!"

When Ah Seow meet him at the well to report the three win, two lost matches, he don't care, he blow, "The sky has at last open the eyes for me!" Dramatically with hands held sky-high, copying the words of the desperate Chap Jee Kee women in their burst of joy when they strikes the number in this illegal lottery.

That evening, in the house with a bamboo deck. Back from the rich man's mansion. He celebrates generously. He brought home three bottles of Pepsi-Cola, a steam chicken worth three dollars, a dollar's worth of assorted meat and vegetables, an apple each for his brothers for dessert. Inviting Kim and Ah Seow to feast together. Kim's father, Ah Hock, a quieter man since Kwang's father died, rubs Kwang's head with his big hand. "Ayaa?" he ask with his ox voice. "Whose big birthday are you celebrating tonight?"

"Eat with us, Uncle Hock . . . !" Kwang evades his question.

Deep down, Uncle Hock at nearly fifty years old with patches of white hair at the side of his ears, was still strong. Was the same man who likes what he likes in his own simple, odd ways. He love his daughter more than gold, what she likes is what he like too. He was engaged at eight, married at eighteen, and didn't have any children until he pray for God's help. He knew Kim and Kwang get along well, he knows what is happening, Kim has told him about Yee when he arrived home. He already had his daily bottle of Guinness stout. He smile and walk back to his room to read Chinese picture comics.

During the feast, it was all spider talks about a big return match with Chai the next day.

Ah Seow said, "You spend so much on food today—you have enough for matching tomorrow?"

"What to scare? I still have forty dollars for food from my mother, here . . . !" He smacks his pocket a few times.

"Don't borrow from me again!" said Kim who runs the washing, marketing, and cooking for Ah Seow and for Ah Hock who works as a cargo laborer.

"Don't worry," Kwang grin. "I can now catch Panther Tiger any time I like. This time sure to win back."

Ah Seow ask, "How many matches tomorrow?"

"Seven all together."

"Late night at the temple tonight," Ah Seow said. "We go and spread the news at the playground. Blind Man is telling stories tonight."

Kwang's kid brothers want to go for stories. Kim act on impulse. She stood up with two rubber bands and tie up her jet-black hair into a ponytail and said, "I go and ask my girlfriends to come. . . . You and Ah Seow go and wash the dishes. Wait awhile for me." And long leg off in her flowery, baggy, samfoo pants.

Ah Seow has a psychic sense developed from ghost and fairy tales in the village. He is afraid of the dark. He went into his room for a six-inches nail under his bed for defense against Pontianak spirits who are suppose to love eating boys' balls.

That night, in the temple courtyard under a basotto tree, Blind Man said, "Even a small boy can make a wild tiger in the jungle run away."

They chorus, "How?"

"First of all"—he cough lightly and raise a finger—"the boy must carry an umbrella. Must be brave when he meets the tiger in the jungle . . . he must remember . . . all tigers will pause to study victims for a while before attacking . . . just like all animals. So, slowly and steadily . . . the boy must pace forward, step by steps with the umbrella open a little, and close . . . open a little bigger . . . and close, bigger and close, bigger and close as he advance closer to puzzle the thinking tiger's attention—and *Whoom!* Blast the umbrella fully open suddenly with a hard scream about ten steps away!" Demonstrating the full blast at the giggling listeners.

"That will make tiger run like a rabbit." And sips his tea to relax and listen to the chattering discussion among themselves before he tell another story, about the Three Foxy Sisters.

In between the stories, Ah Seow and his boss took off to the playground by the old banyan tree which is more busy with older boys and adults, strolling, talking, or eating food sold by gypsy hawkers shouldering their wares on bamboo poles with sizzling rock-gas lights flickering about as they move under full moon. Changing the breathing space of the village into a night market on Kuan Yin Temple's late night on first and fifteenth day of the lunar calendar.

Kwang's sudden appearance surprise spider boys from different sides. Many crowd around him and Ah Seow for information. They tell their faithful supporters to spread the matching news for the next day. Tell those who don't take sides. Stirring up the occasion, boasting about Kwang's new spiders in the campaign to beat their psychological war drums for a big return match.

That night Kwang toss on his bed to dream of winning much glory and a lot of money at the annual Spider Olympic Games. Every year, spider boys within a district match out among themselves for three spiders to participate. Last year's winner also wins the right to hold the grand game in their territory for the following year. Ho Swee Hill has no such honor in its history. Last year winner was the Redhill boys, Changi boys second. Kwang's spider was knocked out in the semifinal. That alone makes him popular overnight, wins the respect of all the spider boys in the whole village, the respect of Chai, son of Big Head and spider voice of the gambling den operator.

They were best friends until the end of last year, when a joke developed into abusive words at the playground, watched by many spider boys. Kwang called Chai's grandmother, Ah Paw, a witch. Chai called Kwang madman's son. And Kwang pounce at Chai in a sudden attack madly, caught the taller and heavier Chai by surprise. They fought like mad dogs until they both roll down the slopes to busy walk path near the temple. Takes two men to tear them apart. Spider boys call it a draw.

The swollen face of black eyes, blood lips, bee-stung nose from Chai's punches didn't receive any sympathy from Kwang's mother. She give him a second hiding. As far as she is concern, don't study hard is bad, fighting is wrong, playing with spiders is worst.

Serious spider boys that number more than a few hundred in the village were split into two groups, and more start to talk good about Kwang, mainly because Chai has monopolize spider business for too long. Cash-rich Chai, the expert in picking winners, has been buying expensive spiders from elsewhere to knock Kwang's out. Economic pressure of losing all the time makes many of Kwang's supporters walk out on him, some join the middle path and don't take sides, turn into an independent third party.

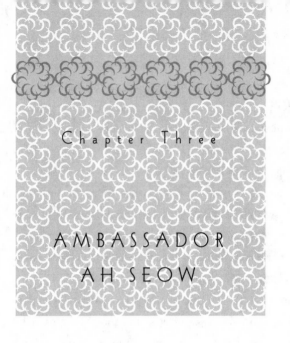

Chapter Three

AMBASSADOR
AH SEOW

Free from mother rule. Early next Sunday morning at the bamboo deck, Kwang takes his spiders out for a war dance under his magnifying glass to grade them. "Don't disturb me!" He wave his little brother away. "I give you all twenty cents each to eat what you want."

Ah Seow ask his boss, "What time do you want the matches to start at the playground?"

"Any time after twelve noon," the boss reply. "If Chai agree."

Like an ambassador, Ah Seow went to see Chai's deputy, San, the son of Wong, a calligrapher, to arrange the time.

Alongside Wong's house, on a corner near the heart of the village, was a wet herbalist, a dry herbalist, a wooden-tong maker, birdcage maker, coppersmith, pot maker, a tailor shop, and a barber shop.

Wong's house has a small shed with hanging pots of orchids spread with charcoal chips to help them bloom. From outside, Ah Seow, a nervous character, saw Wong grinding an ink chalk in a marble bowl on his working table by a window which has the commanding view of the compact village. He hesitates before knocking on the opened door and nods politely.

"Morning, Uncle Wong . . . ! Is San home?"

"San just went out to buy a mug of coffee, sit down and wait for a while." Wong gestures with his head to a long cane settee behind him. And turns back to grind his ink, adding a little water at a time, serenely in his office and living room combined.

The serenity of the old calligrapher make Ah Seow feel at ease. He shifts to the end of the settee for a better view and saw Wong straighten himself with a deep breath. And in one continuous stroke weave out a picturesque word, Dragon, with his brush on a square foot of red paper.

Ah Seow tiptoe forward to watch. "Waah . . . !" he exclaims softly at the word perfectly centered on the red paper, alive with fury and vitality. "Uncle Wong," he ask. "How much you sell a word like that?"

"Depends on the angpow [gift money] from the marrying couple. The next word will be Phoenix," Wong said and lay down his brush to stick a cigarette on his lips, throwing a stream of smoke out of the window like Ah Seow's imaginary dragon come to life.

Ah Seow's curiosity was broken by San's greeting. "Hey...! Ah Seow, what is the new news?" Holding a tin of coffee in a condense milk can dangling on straw ropes and toast bread spread with kayam gravy wrap up in newspaper.

Ah Seow wink an eye with hands imaging spiders wrestling at San who has a pleasant face like his father, looks like he was thinking when he was talking.

San put the coffee and bread on top of chest of drawers besides Wong's working table. "Don't worry about him," he pat his old man. "We can talk about anything in front of him. My father knows everything in the world."

The man of the village twist his son's ear playfully. "The last person I want to blow horn for me is you." He grin behind his thick glasses like dragon eyes to Ah Seow.

Ah Seow was impressed, glad to have attentions. He worship the dragon. Before he could find words to poke around for curiosity, Wong said to him, "Bet fifty cents for me on the last match."

It blows Ah Seow's mind with delight. "Real or not real, Uncle Wong!"

Dragon Wong took the change return from his son's takeaway. "I am not joking with you." He push the coins into Ah Seow's hand. "This world is make for people to see. Money is make to be use." Playfully serious about it.

With the coin magnetize in his hands, without feeling generation gaps, Ah Seow ask, "Why don't you bet on San's side?"

"My son can see near, cannot see far," Wong reply and return to his world of brushing big words for ceremony occasions to make a peaceful living.

Outside, Ah Seow said straightaway, "My boss want to have seven matches today. . . . You think Chai will be ready by twelve o'clock?"

"Twelve o'clock is good time. Betting big?"

"Easily more than ten dollars a match."

"That will be a fight. . . . Chai will be waiting for it," San said. "Ha, good for us too."

"We both know that," Ah Seow smile back. "Shall we go and see Chai together to confirm the time?"

Like close friend and only few months older, San offer him a sweet from his pocket. They both cut corners among narrow lanes into the jungle of the most compact part of the village. Every time they see familiar faces of spider boys, they sell out their voice loudly. "Twelve o'clock! Twelve o'clock!" with a cross sign with fingers to make sure they see the time.

The heart of the village never stops. Fatty's Family, a gang of nine, cook around the clock making cakes. Somebody doing this and that, somebody stirring fine coconut chips marinated in brown sugar with pandan leaves slowly in a giant wok on top of a clay stove with slow-burning charcoal fire. The amazing smells of pandan leaves make their nose sniff, their stomach hungry. "Them good good smells!" San sniff his nose a few times. "Want to eat?" he encourage Ah Seow.

At a three-wheel cart in charge by Fatty's fat sister, Ah Seow spend ten cents on steam glutinous rice surrounded by fine coconut chips tenderly moisturized by brown sugar wrap up in banana leaves. San spend ten cents on nine-color, nine-layer, nine-tastes rice cake. With the hot cakes in their hands, they find a corner to squat down. Ah Seow smells the aroma of pandan leaves first and eat it slowly. San peels his colorful cake, one layer after another into his mouth.

After the feed they went straight to Chai's house attached to his father's gambling den behind the big banyan tree, isolated from other houses in the private area which Big Head's mother, Ah Paw, exorcised with blood of black dog twelve years ago.

The gambling den has corrugated iron roof. Outside the entrance was a patch of hard dry red earth with men wearing undershirts or shirtless, revealing tattoos, chattering away time in a relaxed mood, some listening to the merbok birds singing in their cages. Big Head was rocking comfortably on a lazy rattan chair by the entrance, puffing a pipe, soaking the 9:00 A.M. sunlight like he is taking notice of nothing, except thinking something in his already bald head with one eyebrow divided into two parts by an old knife wound. Wearing a pajama trouser without a shirt, on his chest the old-fashion tattoo of Naja, the child-god warrior.

"Chai's father . . . !" Ah Seow whisper nervously.

"Don't worry about him," San whisper in a low voice. "Just walk straight in, he is half asleep."

Inside the gambling den is one big concrete floor with a large concrete tank in the center, trapping rainwater from an opening on the corrugated roof. The half-dozen full-up ashtrays on the bigger bean-guessing fantan table speak for itself that last night was busy. Out of the five mah-jongg tables, only one is operating in the far corner, with four tired-looking men puffing cigarettes on their lips, swimming their hands on the mah-jongg chips with clashing sounds. And build four walls for another game. They pay no attention to Chai's grandmother, Ah Paw, saturated with crinkles netting her face like an old owl in black samfoo, moving like she was about to fall around their table to empty their ashtrays into a bucket. "Midnight ghosts . . . !" San comment to Ah Seow at those men mah-jongging throughout the night with smokes floating around them in the dim corner.

"That old woman is . . . ?" Ah Seow point nervously at the tiny old witchy figure whose back was hunch down like camel hump.

"Chai's grandmother," San whisper back. "She is deaf, her eyes is very sharp. . . ."

True. The Old Owl's eyes never dies. She saw the boys and start to gallop on wooden thongs toward them with a roll-up cigarette on her lips and a bucket in her hand. "San . . . !" she squeaks. "So early this morning? Chai is still sleeping. He treats the days like the nights . . . !" Drumming up her squeaky voice with cigarette on her lips and lively eyes casting on Ah Seow. And hunchback back to her work.

The boys were standing in front of a table with "free for all" hot tea insulated inside a rattan casing beside small cups in a bucket of water. San pats on Seow's shoulder. "Pour yourself a cup of tea, sit down for a while and wait for me." And walk to the back door.

Ah Seow sits down on the bamboo bench reluctantly to watch his friend disappear into the back door behind a three-feet-high tank in the middle of the gambling hall.

To kill time, Ah Seow stare up dreamily at doorway shrine with a half-life-size colored poster of the Three War Gods of Blood Brotherhood. Pondering on one of the Blind Man's stories that says, "Black face Chang Fei is full of brawls with little brains. Red face Kwan Kung has brain and brawls but not cunning. Pale face Lu Pei is less brawls but very cunning brain to become the King of the Chu Dynasty through their great blood brotherhood spirit."

Ah Seow was totally unaware that old Ah Paw has arrived quietly beside him. She squeaks, "Have you eaten breakfast yet?" With her cigarette on her crinkle thin lips.

Shocked Ah Seow answer meekly, "Eat already."

She watch Ah Seow's lip and edge close. "Hmmm . . . what you eat? Talk in my ears . . . !" She squeak louder, "I am deaf!"

He stammer, "I, I eat a steam cake with sugar coconut."

"Aaaa, from Fatty's Family?" She guess closely and touch Ah Seow's cheek.

Coward Ah Seow freeze a shiver and look downward awkwardly.

"Chaaay . . . !" she scold. "You are useless . . . ! You have no guts, where is your balls?" And start to fiddle around his balls.

Feelings of Pontianak fiend stirs his imagination. "No, can't be in the daytime," he told himself and calm down logically. And glides away from her on the smooth bamboo bench.

She become bold, she wouldn't let go, she grab his shorts and pull closer to hug him. Ah Seow turn stone stiff and let her do what she like. She spit her cigarette butt into her bucket to talk lips to lips. "I like to eat Fatty Family's cake. You look, take a look. I am like a baby, I have no teeth, give me a kiss." And she kiss him.

Her cigarette stench plus bad breath rose up into his nose which cause him to blinks and shakes head to fight for control over himself. She seems to read Ah Seow like a book. Every time he blinks and shakes, she seal it with a stenchy kiss which make Ah Seow let her do what she like with no more control left. She knows it too, nothing escape her eye, she witch-face at him to scare more. And fondle and dig inside his elastic shorts like she was young again with a nickname called Little Chili for her orgies with victims she like in her pirate days.

Her personality change. She point at the tank. "That thing is deep inside the ground. . . . At night you can see the moon making a big pearl inside. Be good to me I will show you my children inside." With eyes shooting out delight and drag a shoulder taller Ah Seow to the tank.

Spellbounded Ah Seow absorb every word she say. And obey. On arrival, she touch a hand on the edge of the tank which drops another six feet deep below ground level, and said romantically, "Look inside first."

Robot Ah Seow look.

"I show you my childrens." She squeak grumpily and sweeps the weedy water once.

A pair of carp fish about three feets long, black and orange in colors, swim up before Ah Seow's shocked eyes.

She sweeps the water together with two hands, twice.

Three big fat fluffy fins and tails goldfishes size like newborn puppies swim up.

She tiptoe higher and butterflies her hand on the water surface. The three goldfish swim toward her fingers, nibbling. The two carp fishes rubs their scaly body cuddly against her hand. "This is the male, this is the female." She point at the carps' heads. "They are older than youngest grandson Chai, they are like dogs, they have good sense, they know me very well. That three naughty goldfishes is no good, belong to my useless son that Old Substance. They come to me only for foods!"

True. The moment she speaks, the three goldfishes swim away.

She dips her hands deeper to rub the bellies of the carp fish couple. Their relationship spellbounded a fairy tale into the mystic and carry Ah Seow away into the watery world, as if he heard the fish speaking.

"What do you think that boy thinks of us, darling?" says the female carp.

"Darling!" the male carp say. "You always ask the same questions when you see somebody new. Can't you see? It is all about curiosity. No difference, really. He wants to know you like you want to know him."

Female carp ask, "Don't you think it is boring doing the same things? All the time?"

The three goldfishes swim up and sing, "Just-t be-ee grate-ee-ful! For what-tt you have . . . ! No-ooo boo-dy is eat-ee-ing us . . . !"

Male carp say, "Yes, yes, I agree."

"You mean be here now?" ask the talkative female.

"Exactly . . . ! Just relax! Why don't you stop talking?"

"Darling . . . ! My fish brain is not born like that!" she reply and ask three goldfish, "What you all think?"

"Pay no attention to the old woman!" they advise together and dive deeper into the milky depths of the weedy water.

"Ah Seow!" Chai's husky voice boom out behind San through the back door below the Three War Gods. Pushing his bicycle decorated with film stars cut out and pasted on it.

Ah Paw click clocks away on her wooden thongs with a sideways glance at her nearly fourteen years old grandson. He looks like his father in every aspect; bulky and big head, short stubby leg, long thick body, and short thick neck. Shooting up as tall as the average man. He start to make his own living at nine years old through wrestling spiders and bought his own bicycle at ten.

"Ah Seow," San ask with a wink. "What are you doing here? Let's go outside first."

Ah Seow, fresh from his mystical experience, follows them out rubbing his short hairs. As if he woke up from a bad dream.

Outside the main intersection of the village, Chai stop his bicycle and lean against it. "Ah Seow . . . !" He frown with fresh pimples on his broad face. "Next time you come to my house, don't talk to my grandmother, okay?"

Ah Seow didn't like to be treated like that by the opposition leader. He turn to San and said, "She is very strange, crazy?" To irritate Chai.

"Something wrong, like your name," Chai shoot straight. "Everybody in my house is crazy and strange. My grandmother is worst . . . ! She think she is a little girl and like boys."

"In the daytime is not so bad," San said. "At night . . . she will try to take off your trousers. . . . The main thing is you must not be scare of her."

"Alright, alright, don't talk about my grandmother . . . !" Chai rubs his hand. "Ah Seow, let's talk money first. Did you say your boss is betting big today?"

Ah Seow blow. "More than fifty dollars himself. Can you handle that?"

"Any more?" Chai lift up his round chin.

Ah Seow seize the opportunity. "That means the match is on. Seven matches from twelve noon?"

Chai sweep a look at San. San make a slight nod. "Okay . . . !" Chai said. "Make it twelve to twelve-thirty. San, tell our side to ready for our sure to win show first." He pull out a short comb from the back pocket of his tailor-made shorts to comb his weak hairs backward, left and right.

At the bamboo deck, Kwang's brothers were playing cards with casing of cigarette boxes as currencies, with a group of small kids. "Rare brands worth more" was their system of evaluating their money market which fluctuates according to supply and demand. Learning basic mathematics through gambling. Sometimes two Cat brand casings is worth five cents, can buy an otak cake which Kwang's brothers are eating with one hand as they play cards with other hand. Or, one Cat brand is worth ten Navy Cut brand.

Below the round table on the deck, Kwang was teasing a Mr. Spider vibrating around a Miss under his thumb on a spider box. Kim was eyeing the actions with his magnifying glass above spiders closely. "Look, look." She butts her head at Kwang's and giggles. "Look at their desperate faces, look . . . !"

"Saw the male's stick thickening?" he ask and nip at the bud of her flowering breast and withdraw like a whip.

"Don't do it here . . . !" She wince with her always ready to laugh eyes bigger. And concentrate to watch the magnified white-face male spider flippering helplessly to free the black-face female. Keen to learn what a female spider do to attract the male like crazy. Regardless of how long Kwang's thumb mount on top of her, the male will try to free her. And Kim knows it. Because she has seen Kwang pressing the female's behind for hours to observe spiders, and yet once free, the male will screw her nonstop. Such fantasies do get into her head.

Ambassador Ah Seow step up the bamboo deck and reports. "Everything is arrange, Chai agree on twelve to twelve-thirty."

"Okay, good," Kwang reply and continue frustrating the male for another five-minute session before he separate the spiders into two different boxes. Then scratches three stripes on the corner of the surface with a coin to rank the male spider. And pass it to his assistant. "Na, Ah Seow."

Kim elbow at Kwang. "Why don't you let them live in the same box together?"

"It is a trick . . . ! Make male think about the female and angry at other males when the matching starts. If win? I will let them stay together again." Eyeball to eyeball at her, at her always ready to laugh almond eyes that melts him down, that knocks him left and right all the time because it came out of his own soul, came from laughing at his odd looks since growing up. And was warm and naughty, because she felt pity at the way his mother beat him up.

"Why!" She butt her forehead against his.

"Why?" he said. "I know everything about my Panther Tigers."

"I want to make some money today. . . . What time the match start?" she ask and lean backward in her light cotton T-shirt.

Feeling a bit left out by their renewed intimacy, Ah Seow said loudly for attention, "Twelve to twelve-thirty!"

Kwang stretch out his hands and look at the sun and yawn. "Woh . . . ! Eleven o'clock already! Hey Kim, what about ask all your girlfriends to come? This time Chai will surely die." With a wink at Ah Seow for support.

"Yes . . . !" Ah Seow sell. "The more people on our side the better, Chai has more money and people than us. Double the money with five cents can make a lot."

"Don't make me lose face . . . !" she warn Kwang with a finger like a tomboy and walk away to gather her girlfriends over.

Ah Seow went into his room to count money and prepare the paperwork for the match. Kwang continued to warm up his spiders.

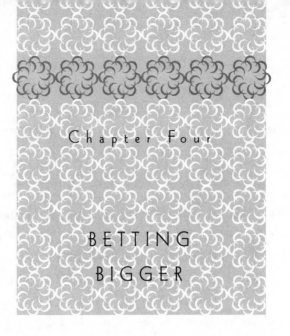

Chapter Four

BETTING
BIGGER

Tomboy Kim was a popular girl in the village. She brought back more than a dozen girls about her age.

Ah Seow was thrill. He ask them, "You all know how to bet?"

"Don't know...!" a talkative girl said. "Your sister pull us here!"

"Easy...!" said Ah Seow with a pencil and a record book. "Better play kongsi [partnership], five cents a share. We pool the money together, divide the shares later. Sometimes five cents can make more than one dollar in the seven matches today . . . !" to the puzzle-face girls who crowd around him. He teach them mathematics patiently until those girls nod their heads and call him smart. Ah Seow was delighted from all the total attention give to him by the girls. Girls save harder than boys, some girls bought ten shares.

Talkative girl ask again, "How long we have to wait?"

"We go now!" Ah Seow exclaims in a jovial mood from a sense of importance. And lead the way with a schoolbag over his shoulder with all the spiders and a betting record book inside. Kim piggyback Kwang, then Kwang piggyback Kim and follow behind.

Their playground center around the huge old banyan tree, usually quiet in the midafternoon, was busy with spider boys. When the girls arrive, those boys wonder why. All their heads turn. A boy in Chai's larger team said, "Aaaya? They bring girls to show off . . . !"

Another boy said to him who has many sister, "Don't lose face, ask your sisters to bring their girlfriends."

"Go . . . go, don't lose face," San encourage him.

"Okay, okay," he agree with a skippy smile and took off.

Kwang's boys were already waiting by a hollow in the banyan which has a small shrine for Da Bo Gong, the Grandfather God who bless the poor. They crowds around Ah Seow who took down names and collects shares with receipts for pool betting. Without mother's rule, Kwang feel positive. "Don't worry," he encourage them. "Gamble out your guts today . . . !"

"Girls also dare to play . . . !" Ah Seow back up his boss to encourage more bets as he counts the coins and double-check.

The third party who don't take sides gathers around the usual wrestling spider arena on the edges of the banyan with old roots dropping down to form baby trees. Boys and girls start to swap words and roast up the atmosphere. Kim was smelling the occasion with deep dimple smiles. More independent boys start to crowd around their team.

Just past noon. More spider boys arrived. Just before twelve-thirty Chai arrived with bicycle bell ringing on his bike. A dashing figure. He dismount and let his bike sleep flat on his patch, pass his shoulder bag to San, pull out his short comb and combs his hair backward left and right. "Hey, San, what are those girls here for?"

"They come to bet with money," a spy report.

"Big betting today," San said.

"That is better," Chai fiddles the teeth of his comb. "We will dry out all their pockets today."

San ask, "You brought any new spiders today?"

"Don't worry," Chai slip the comb in his back pocket. "All are conquerors from Redhill and Pasir Panjang."

Ah Seow walk over and call out at a distance, "San! Want to set up the table now?"

"Up to you!" San shout back.

From a hollow around the main tree, they took out the gear for staging the matches. And clap hands to wave their team to the wrestling spider arena at the edge of the shade. The space was flat and spacious, which is just nice, not too dim like the center of the tree thick with leaves and buttress trunks crawling all over the ground.

The boy with many sisters also bring lots of girls. Nearly two hundred boys and girls quickly jostle around the arena with both referees shouting, "Tew chiam! Tew chiam! [Take your pick!] Red on the front! Blue, white, green follow behind!" Using color satay sticks in a tin, they lottery out their viewing position.

Tomboy Kim pushes away the boys. "Girls sit in front!" she demand. Boys feel embarrass to quarrel with girls, they make way, girls take the front rows. Kim squats beside Kwang. It didn't take long for them to pack like sardines in a crater formation, front rows squatting, back-up kneeling and half squatting with hands on their knees, follow by standings, jostling in their commotion at the spider ring, a smooth brick-size block on a meter-square plywood supported by four other blocks.

Referee San rings a brass bell. Commotions stop.

Opposite the arena the two chiefs calmly pull out spider boxes from their bags and hold them up to please the crowd. Referee Seow spin a coin to decide who starts.

Chai combs his big head and said, "Head . . . !"

It was tail.

"Wrong guess!" Ah Seow point at Chai in a refereelike manner. "You start!"

Chai took out a packet of Navy Cut brand cigarette and a lighter from his big side pocket shirt and place it on the plywood coolly, sought out a spider box from his shoulder bag and pass it to Ah Seow. Ah Seow let out that spider to walk about on the smooth white block for public display.

Referee San point at Kwang. "You want to weight?"

Kwang snaps his finger at Chai's spider as he block it path, spider jump onto his palm, he feel the weight, the force of spider's jumping and landing between his two hands. "Enough," he said coldly and handed it back to referee San. And search out a box from his bag. "Kim . . . give it to him," he thumb at San.

Kim snatch it with a lousy look at Chai and hand it to San.

San let it out to walk about for a public display on the block.

"Enough?" Ah Seow ask the public. There was no complaints. "Your turn to weight," Ah Seow said to Chai authoritatively.

Chai waves a middle finger in front of the face of Kwang's spider like saying, "Get fuck, get fuck," for it to jump on his hand and make the audience laugh, irritating his opposition as he weight and study it with a quick glance at Kim. Kim give him another lousy look. Kwang stay cool with his arms fold.

"Kombang! Kombang!" Ah Seow rings the bell for betting time.

Referee San announce the matching rules. "Seven matches today! Unless banker bankrupt . . . !"

"Chai? Your call . . . !" referee Seow said.

Cash-rich Chai took out a bundle of one-dollar notes from his bag and lay it on the plywood, licks his hand and peel out dollar by dollar to float on the table slowly. "Twenty dollars," he said with an air of a poker player to annoy and raid his rival's capital in a tactical move.

Plus his own money and more than fifty crews averaging twenty cents each, Kwang has more than twenty dollars in the pool capital. "Eight dollars for a start . . . Leave some for others to play," he said coolly as he counted the coins and give to Kim.

Kim sucks her full lips and push the coins to the center.

Chai light a cigarette with a puff at the money on the table.

Ah Seow recounts the money and said, "San, twelve dollars left."

San stood up to ring his bell and announce, "Twelve dollars extra! Twelve dollars on the table for public bet! Any challenge! Any more challenge!" And squat down to pile the cash aside.

"Come on! Come on!" Ah Seow stood up and claps. "Quick hands make a move before betting close! Before betting close!"

From the independent party some shout, "Five cents!" some, "Ten cents!" And both referees stand up to collect bets and issue receipts which total nine dollars and push the balance of three dollars back to Chai.

Referee San rings a bell.

Referee Seow signal, "Start!" with a chop above the brick-size white block of wood on the meter-square plywood.

Both chiefs aim their spider on the block with a gentle flick at its tail. Both spiders jump into the ring to face each other.

Kwang's spider is tattooed in spots and stripes of silvery deep purple, Chai's in silvery dark turquoise. At the sight of each other, both wrestling spiders stretch out their arms like wings apart for action, head down, body up with two fans curve inward tightly as if to say, "Get out of my way or else!"

After a fury stare they charge at each other and war-dance backward and forward with arms apart floatingly. Purple shift a step backward, Turquoise move a step forward. Purple move forward, Turquoise move backward. Both shifting forward and backward closer and closer simultaneously in slow motion, tempting each other to make a mistake in a hypnotic war dance. Purple hold his ground, Turquoise attack. Purple counterattack, clashing with arms hammering, tusk teeth grinding, face butting at each other in a half-crawling position. Then! In a sudden switch of actions faster than the eyes could follow, they both stood up on hind legs at an angle of forty-five degrees to lock jaws, arms and legs pounding at each other at vibrating speed faster and faster in a battle of strength. Like warriors in psychedelic armor under the blinking eyes of boys and girls. Seconds later, both tumble down together in a crumble, crumbling and tumbling on top of each other a few times, then burst apart to struggle up and dance and clash again.

Every time they separate and come together to fight again, spider boys call it one round. This happen only in a good fight. After three rounds, Chai's Turquoise run away with an injured leg, Kwang's team roar with joy, clapping their hands for the first goal score.

An hour has passed in five matches. Kwang's team lost only one match, their capital has triple. Independent party also wins a lot. At the opening of the sixth match, Chai's thick dollars and coins were all gone. He didn't bother to comb his hairs, he wipes the sweats from his forehead on his shorts, fumbles to unzip his back pocket for his purse to take out a layer of red ten-dollar notes and slams it hard on the plywood table. "Monkey Boy . . . !" he nickname Kwang for the first time. "Today is the day for you to take revenge, got the guts, do me a favor . . . ! Bet bigger!" And stick a cigarette on his lips.

The crowd turn silence.

"What do you want!" Kwang suddenly slams harder back on the plywood and stood up to face Chai like spiders ready for a fight.

"Go back! Go back!" Kim intervene with two hands against their chests. "Like that . . . ! I want to go home now . . . !"

Kwang calms down, Chai calms down. Referees reset the gear.

Chai takes up his red crispy notes to straighten and fans out like cards in his hand to compose himself. "More than a hundred here." He spread it on the table. "If you have enough guts—take it and eat." And took out his sixth spider, a dark blue one.

Kwang edge down his head to think awhile and said quietly, "Okay, lah . . . Referees . . . count his money." And untie the rubber band under his pocket to take out his mother's forty dollars, food money for a month, throw it on the table at San. "Referee . . . !" he said tensely. "If our pool money is not enough, add this for me in the public bet records." And took out his best spider, a dark purple.

In the sixth match the two great spiders never let anybody down. They fought from crawling position to standing and lock jaws, crumble and tumbles together, break loose, war dance, clash again, crumble and break loose. One round, two rounds, three rounds vigorously, until six rounds, they both tire, but like great warriors, they fought on! Hypnotizing everybody to a frenzy, heads and body swaying without a blink at wrestling spiders in action on a block of wood, ecstatically.

The dripping sweats of the sardined boys and girls packed together in the afternoon heat smells like nothing to anybody, intensify the excitement. Except for the referees who have to keep calm. Ah Seow felt exotic with all the girls in the front rows around him, he caught San stealing eye at his sister's growing nipples transparent through her soaking-wet light cotton T-shirt. Kim grip Kwang's hand so tight, her fingernails bites into his flesh, he can't feel the pains, he tighten his teeth to watch with thoughts of a month of mother's food money at risk.

At the seventh round they didn't war dance, they crawl to meet, clashing tiredly at reduce speed in a flat position. With a heave, Kwang's toss the Dark Blue of Chai into a back flip, it scramble up with a giddy look and run for his life. The audience roars and gasps into silence with a sense of relief for winning and pains for losing.

Kwang took his prized spider in his palm and spit saliva for him to drink. Ah Seow's hand was shaking when he counts the dollars. San keep the defeated spider tenderly. Chai light up a smoke and comb his hair slowly to compose himself. "Monkey Boy," he put up a brave face, "today is your day, is your money. You clean me out."

Kwang reply, "I give you a return match anytime you want."

"Chai...!" the talkative girl call out in a sympathy voice. "Chai...! Where are you going?"

Chai didn't reply. He walk away with his familiar spider bag on his shoulder, hanging down his head, refusing to look at the equally sad face of his team, and ride his bicycle away.

Chai's team drift away in separate directions with their own spider future in their mind.

Kwang's team walk in unity to celebrate an open-house party at his house. Some independent party join them.

San and Ah Seow stay back to divide their referee's 5 percent commission on the day's betting turnover and pack up the simple spider gear for storage. "Lucky," San said, "I took my father's hint and bet on your side behind Chai's back."

"Not easy to make Chai's money," Ah Seow reply.

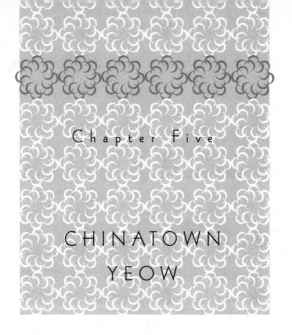

Chapter Five

CHINATOWN
YEOW

Chai went home to toss between selling his bicycle or to steal money from his grandmother. Finally he decided to see Chinatown Yeow for a loan.

Smiling-face Yeow came from Penang. His parents disappeared during the Japanese occupation. An aunt who brought him up died when he was seven years old. He join street boys left over by war, scraping for food, got bully like anybody in the beginning. At nine years old, he saw a snatch thief doing a hit-and-run job.

He told one of the older boys, "We can do the same thing . . . !"

"We too small," older boy said. "Can't run fast enough."

"Help me talk to the bigger boys, lah," Yeow insists.

A bigger boy said, "I can do the running, what can you do?"

"Spy rich people," he reply.

More talking turn into actions. The first successful job inspire others, some get caught. They learn, learn to exchange informations, about trust, about keeping their mouth shut, dress well to surprise victims as they change tactics.

When Yeow tosses around to sleep, he enjoy screening the faces of victims screaming for help while his mates ran away with the loot, smilingly. Resenting bitterly at the faces of rat wars within his own kind for scraps, the unfair dividends, the bullying, jealousy, and division. Like a movie. The whole movie replay again and again make him think harder to avoid conflict. Survival instinct make him know his own strength and weakness. He sort the good and bad behind a smiling face that helps him do better than the rest.

Privately a lone wolf. He digs his past to find the future. Every time he hear the voice of old women hawking noodles, "Chee cheong fan . . . ! Chee cheong fan!" late in the night, like howling with two heavy buckets of food on their shoulder with bamboo poles. Such voice and image remind him of his dead auntie who sells the same food in the same way. It chokes him up, powers him with ambitions. He developed photographic memory from keen sense of spying on people and places. Yeow's spying was quality. He supply his informations to the best snatchers according to his own judgment.

Four years of spying turn him into thirteen years old as he shoots taller at that age. "Why don't you do a bigger job?" he ask an old-timer snatcher who has graduated from street life to become a member of the Siew Jee Ho secret society, but still has a snatch thief habit.

"No loopholes, you have any?" Old-timer reply. "Anything happen not your problems. Tell me, I give you a fair cut."

"I trust you. You are quickest." Yeow smile at the twenty years Old-timer who only failed twice in his seven-year career.

"Talk it out, lah, Smiling Boy," Old-timer wink with an arm round Yeow's shoulder.

"All the rich women go to the Po Heng Goldsmith shop, the boss is a woman, very very rich. . . . I know how many times she go to the bank in a week. . . . Two times . . . !" Yeow gesture with two finger. "She drive to the bank from her big house in a quiet place. Catch her at her own doorstep . . . you know what I mean . . . ?"

"That is easy . . . !" Old-timer snap his fingers and offer 30 percent. "Three cut for you. You do the lookout, okay?"

"Talk at the seaside, lah," Yeow smile. "More quiet . . . I like the breeze." They draw their plans on the sandy beach.

That job came out in the newspaper. The reported loss was more than twenty thousand dollars. Old-timer disappeared with the money. From that day, Yeow was bitter and cannot sleep, keep asking himself, "What else can I be . . . ? I cannot read. I cannot write. No real friends. Nothing! If I am like that all the time . . . I might as well die! Where is my guts?" He wake up from his nightmares and blink his eyes to replay the movies of his life, every night, like a hungry lone wolf tortured by a new voice for vengeance at growing age.

Yeow remember Old-timer talks about the nightclubs and bar girls of Kuala Lumpur. He also remember the popular saying in secret societies, "Nobody is born brave. If you want to come out to roam, you must be, dare to be." He starts to jog and train up his stamina. Within a few months he executed a case which net him a few hundred dollars all alone. Without telling anybody and a few pieces of clothing in a shoulder bag, he catch a ferry and a train on a 250-miles trip to Kuala Lumpur for the first time. Too young to check into a hotel which requires identity card created by British against Communists recruiting members, he sleep in BB Park on starry nights and on the benches of Kuala Lumpur Railway Station on cloudy nights. Mapping around the new environment with his photographic mind in the mornings.

With Old-timer's habit in mind, with the skill of a spy, he scout around popular food streets in afternoons and evenings, watching outside the bars and nightclubs by nights.

In Batta Road of Bukit Bintang at the heart of Kuala Lumpur, he saw him eating the best food. Yeow tail him to his flat, patiently, watch his habits, watch him going to the bars on the main streets of Bukit Bintang and brought home different bar girls almost every night. One night, at a distance, Yeow saw him stagger out of the bar alone after closing time, drunk. "So you can't fuck every night?" Yeow bitter smile and ran ahead of him.

He climb into his flat on the second floor via the vertical water pipes close to the balcony near midnight, and hide under his bed, and wait. The moment he hears the key unlock the door, he steady his nerve with a bearing scraper against his chest and think like a man in a trance. "Is either you or me. . . . Is either you or me." Chanting to steady his nerve. When the drunken guy was snoring, he crawl out to look at him and think bitterly, "I have waited, and waited . . . you eat me! I eat you!" He scream inside and plunge the nine-inch blade right through his heart with two hands in one stroke. That guy jerk to hold his chest with eyes and mouth wide. "Can you recognize me?" Yeow said softly to watch him die, watching his tongue shortening into the throat of his open mouth and eyes.

Yeow breathe heavily after the first taste of "revenge is sweet" which strengthen his guts, which give him new sensation of rawness in cold blood. Leaving the bearing scraper on Old-timer's chest, he switch on the light, found his door keys attach to a few small keys on the dressing table, open up the drawers, found no money, look at the dressing table again, pull out the bottom drawer completely and found a false bottom with half of the original money in a plastic bag. Walk out of the flat quietly. Catch the midnight train across the Johore Causeway to Singapore.

In Singapore, Yeow bury his money and walk aimlessly in the streets of Chinatown for a job that can give him a place to stay, even without pay. Nobody want him. Rejected everywhere, sleeping on the streets again make him angry and depressed. A stranger in a new land. The new experience of complete loneliness was the worst, his brains roundabout with questions and answers storming in a whirlpool. The bottomless pit cracks up. It fires him to say, "Yes!" And he join the street boys of Chinatown which numbers a lot more than Penang.

Yeow's blood flows hot with a new vision. With new brains and new guts of a boy who kill a man, six years of street life behind him. Behind a smiling face with money and communication skill, within a few years he organize a unity among scattered street boys by picking up the qualities to control the quantities within a spying network. And capitalize on informations of all kinds under a new mask.

The history of Singapore is fabricated by two lawmakers: the Chinese secret societies who use knives and fists among themselves and the British who rule with guns and wits since 1819. In postwar Singapore, all Chinese business in every street pays protection money. Every street has a gang. Those years was also the years of political parties sprouting up, like the Alliance, Labor, Barisan Socialist, People's Action party led by Lee Kuan Yew. Chinese school students rioting, shouting, "Merdeka! Merdeka! Merdeka!" for independence. Gurkha troops were brought in by the British to stop them. The Communist movement was gaining ground supported by the majority of the poor. The British make new laws. Everybody above twelve years old has to carry an identity card with a photo.

Open gang clashes among secret societies happen every day. Rebels within gangs constantly sprout out to form new gangs. They use numbers to identify their groups, number is strength, is the meaning of their movement. It tune with the time, and was trendy, has a macho appeal for young recruits who like to dress up like teddy boys with skintight pants and get into the sounds of rock and roll or cha-cha of Western music. Many copy Elvis Presley who is known to them as King Cat. The Black and White youth gang wear shirt with collar turned up high, tattoos were changed from dragons and godlike warriors to cowboy girls with big tits, English letters, or animals like black panther and snakes. Some adjust their collar to reveal their gang, some stroke their nose with two fingers to say, "I am from Two-Four," or make a zero sign when light a match, for Zero-Eight gang. One of Chai's half brothers belong to the Two-Four gang, the other belong to the Three-Six-Nine.

When Chai went biking to a popular food stall in Chinatown to locate Yeow he saw a skinny brown girl with a grape-size mole under her left eye, walking with a small nuggety boy three or four years younger than her. "Big Mole! Big Mole!" Chai yell and stop his bike to push toward them. "Big Mole . . . ! Have you seen Yeow?"

Big Mole look at her boy. The boy shakes his chubby face. She stares at Chai's fresh pimples on a broad face. "I don't know," she lie slowly, like counting Chai's pimples to avoid his suspicious gaze. And scratch her scrawny hand on her fuzzy hair.

Big Mole was about Chai's age. He knew the pair well, knew the nuggety boy with spiky crew-cut hair was Yeow's favorite spy. "Na . . . ! Sachee," Chai said briskly, "have a smoke? Don't say I have nothing for you." Taking out a packet of cigarettes to offer him a smoke in a hurry.

Sachee stick it on his lips and wave a finger by the cigarette for a light. Chai flinch a look at Big Mole and light it for him. Sachee blow the smoke in the air. "Big Head Chai, can you spare another ten cents for a cup of coffee?" Flicking away the cigarette ashes like a man.

Chai give him ten cents with a frown. "Na . . . !"

Sachee jerk his thumb backward. "Yeow is in Santeng, listening to Cheong Pak telling newspaper news."

Chai wasted no time and ride away with his bicycle bell ringing in the midst of human traffic in packed Chinatown.

Walking hand in hand, Big Mole stop and said, "Sachee . . . ! Why you point your finger the other way for Big Head Chai to go for a monkey ride? He will be mad the next time he saw us!"

"Why scare? He is not our friend . . . !" Sachee punch his hand. "Do you know he look down on us? Has money and never give us anything? Talk to us only when he want something? I don't like his bully face."

Sachee (Small Stick) was brought up on the back of his grandmother who piggyback him to beg for a living. When he can walk and talk, they beg together. One day he wonder why his grandmother cannot walk and talk. She was dead. He beg his own way up until Yeow saw him begging together with Big Mole and took them under his wing.

Big Mole was the only girl among the street kids of Chinatown. She was a lost Indonesian child found by a prostitute during the Japanese occupation at just-walking age. Run away at around ten from the prostitute who live in a brothel.

Chai took another day to locate Yeow. "Yeow, can you front up fifty dollars for three month? I pay you back at the interest rate."

"I don't make money from friend." Yeow took out his purse and ask, "Is that enough?"

"That is very give face already." Chai rounds his big eyes at him. "I wouldn't forget this favor."

"Just keep the date on time." Yeow baby-smile on his handsome face.

With the borrowed money from Yeow, Chai did alright with his spider business elsewhere, but always lost to Kwang every time he try to win back from him. His team almost abandon him completely. He then spend all his time out of the village to catch up with lost time, come home only to sleep.

One evening at the Chinese Picture Comic rental stall against the long side wall of the Ho San coffee shop at the edge of Chinatown, Yeow was sitting on a stool against the wall under bright pump lamp, smiling occasionally as he turn the comic of Cha Kun the Monk, who love to eat dog meat and yet becomes a saint. Big Mole and Sachee were there too. Sachee was reading Mickey Mouse comics on a stool, next to Big Mole watching the forever busy activities in front of her. She saw Chai. "Sachee, Sachee." She slap quickly on his arm. "Big Head Chai . . . !"

"Where?"

"There . . . !" She jerk her egg chin on a worried face.

Sachee walk a few steps to Yeow who like to sit alone when he is reading comics. "Yeow . . ." He kick quietly at his leg. "That big-head boy is here . . ." and walk back to read his comic.

"Hey . . . ! Yeow!" Chai wave and chain his bike around a post.

"Don't worry about locking it in this area!" Yeow shouts and smile at the way Chai treasure his bike with groovy pictures.

"Keep my words, come to pay you back the money first." Chai comb his hair backward with a mean glance at Big Mole and Sachee. They pretend not to see him. He slip back his comb, took out a packet of cigarette and walk over to Sachee. "Na . . . ! Have a smoke?" To set up Sachee who know Yeow don't like him to smoke.

Sachee snuffs his nose at Chai with a glance at Yeow and bend his spiky crew-cut head down to read Mickey Mouse.

Yeow walk up with a comic in his hand and smack on Sachee's head. "Big man . . . ! When did you start to smoke?"

Sachee look at his comic stubbornly. Big Mole pull her stool nearer to him and bites her fingernail.

"Chai, how is luck?" Yeow pats on his expanding shoulder.

"Don't ask." Chai shakes his head and smokes. "Win everywhere, lost back to the same boy in my village." With a robust voice that begin to sound like his father and bigger than an average man.

"That shark-head boy with a stupid haircut?" Yeow grin.

"You know him!" Chai exclaim.

"Few times," Yeow reply casually and gesture with his head. "Come, let's sit inside the coffee shop, my shout."

Inside the noisy Ho San coffee shop where people talk like a market-place, Chai who knew Yeow on and off ever since he arrive from Penang throw his packet of smoke on the table and take out his purse. "Yeow," he grimace. "My money is still tight, any loopholes?" Counting the notes and pushing them across the table.

Yeow make a brief stare at the money in front of him and rest his hands on the table. "Drink first . . . hot or cold?"

"Strong black coffee." Chai edge forward to pull out his comb, and combs his hair.

"Two, white for me." Yeow raise two fingers at the coffee boy who stand by to serve the moment he saw Yeow. "Chai," Yeow push back the money on the table to him. "Don't be shy with me, take your time and pay me back when you are ready, okay?"

Chai pocket the money and said, "I won't forget this favor. . . . Seen my brothers?"

"No . . . not for a few months. They do their own thing, you?"

"Only my second brother briefly last month . . . at home once."

"How much did you lost to that shark-head boy?"

"Don't want to count," Chai frown. "I am losing face in my own village."

Yeow who is always talent scouting test the water. "You want me to sort him out for you?"

"No . . ." Chai shakes his head and smoke. "Is a one-to-one thing between him and me . . . very hard to explain."

"A lot of things are very hard to explain." Yeow stirs his coffee. "Heard a lot about Ho Swee Hill, I feel like going to your place to see a new world for a change."

"Plenty space, stay at my place any time you like."

"Tomorrow okay?"

"Sure . . . ! I take you on my bicycle from here. What about nine in the morning, too early . . . ?"

"No, early is good." Yeow sips his coffee. "I find a bicycle myself, we ride together." And smile. "More fun."

"Okay, here tomorrow at nine." Chai finished up his coffee and walk out happily to unlock his bicycle. There was no air in both tires. He push his bike to prowl for Big Mole and Sachee fruitlessly. They were watching him around a corner.

Inside the coffee shop, Yeow order another coffee to reflect with Chai and Chai's rival, Kwang, on his mind. He is planning to extend beyond Chinatown. He like Kwang the first time they meet, was impress by the way he beat up one of his own boys in Nam Tain Lane who make Kwang famous among themselves. Although Yeow put on a calm face and has complete control in his expanding territories, he was lonely by generation gaps between himself and his boys who treated him like a father figure, not friend. He was growing into the world of manhood with a vision to do other things ahead of his time. He look a few years older than his eighteen years, and is looking for soul mates who are also leaders themselves.

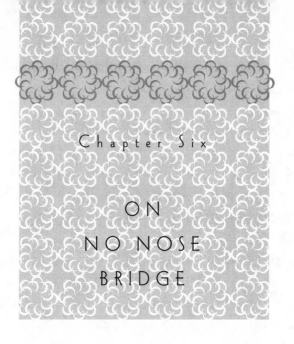

Chapter Six

ON
NO NOSE
BRIDGE

No Nose Bridge. Suspended over the shallow river dividing Ho Swee village from the rest of the outside world, was name after No Nose, the old kite-maker, by his fans. Rubbish dumped throughout the years narrowed the river and formed a basin where nobody stay. It flood in the rainy season and dries up in kite season, becomes the playground of kite fighting activities against the rest of the world on the opposite bank. Kite fighting is a passion game in Singapore. Boys called it cross sword in the sky. Before the sword is ready to fly, the long rows of cotton string is sharpen by glazing, dipping it in boiling ox-skin glue, mixed with pounded powdery glass.

The next morning, in the beginning of the dry windy season, No Nose was testing his kites in the gusty winds with half a dozen man-size boys worshiping around him.

"Woh . . . ! Woh . . . ! Chai!" Yeow rubs his nose. "Chai . . . ! another world!" He stop his bike to push up on the few-meter-wide bouncy bamboo-rafted suspension bridge over the stinking river.

Grim-face Chai chuckle broadly. "You come at the right time, the most stinking time . . . !" As he brakes from behind.

"Most stinking time?" Yeow ask loudly in the gusty morning.

"Always like that!" Chai voice blow louder in the wind. "Kite season's starting! River dries and fucks out at this time!" He stop to talk to his father's friend passing by on the forty-meter-long bridge.

Yeow push his bike ahead slowly as he view the horizon of brown atap roof covering the hilly village from his commanding position left and right and front. He feel high on the bridge, he glance back to look at Chai. Chai was still chatting. Yeow forge ahead and caught the sight of No Nose's sunken face and raggy small figure flying his kite. Yeow stares amused.

No Nose hate outsiders' stares. His nose was slice off during the war by a Japanese officer when he bowed and sneezed. "Don't you know your father?" he insult and backward a few steps to block Yeow's path with a pull of the line anchored round an oval tin, below Yeow's chin, like shooting a bow and arrow with his kite in the sky.

Yeow compose himself with one hand in his pocket, other hand holding the bike and gaze around those faces, his age. Just smile at No Nose's sun-season sunken opium face, scarecrow figure no more than five feet tall. No Nose check Yeow from head to toe. Yeow is average build and symmetrically handsome, his shining black hair is neatly parted with a straight line, very well trimmed. Like always, neatly dress up in white cotton long-sleeve shirt rolled up to his elbow, expensive old-fashion baggy trousers, and leather shoes.

"Eeeh...!" No Nose sniff. "Where do you smell? Got the guts to admit it!" In a hollow tone vibrating from his two holes in his face.

"I don't waste my breath for nothing." Yeow smile at him and turn his head to look for Chai.

No Nose slip the kite line and hold, the glaze line slice into Yeow's chin, he jerk backward and hold the line, No Nose pull the line, the line slice Yeow's hand. At once, No Nose's worshipers shift forward with aggressive face.

Yeow feel like smashing his bike at them but the burst of boiling fury inside stop by itself. He bend his head down to pull out a well-folded handkerchief to bite at one end and bandage his hand, ignoring the worshipers, ignoring the blood dripping down his chin to soak his white shirt. "I have not seen blood before," Yeow said icily. "What is all this for? Do you have to do this to me...?" Showing the bloody handkerchief hand.

No Nose glance at his kite in the sky and backward a step.

Yeow turn around and burst a sudden terrific roar. "Chai!"

Chai throw down his bike and ran forward like a bulldog with his powerfully built long body and short arms and legs. "Yeow? What happen...? Who did it?" he ask around in haste with a bulldog face.

Yeow slow smile at No Nose. "Ask him, ask this little old prick for me. He ask me where I smell. Tell him . . . tell him I don't play with any number. Ask him if he could afford to pay my damage. I am very expensive."

No Nose didn't flinch, he continue to anchor his kite in the same bow-and-arrow position with slight squat knees, tugging the kite lines on and off like fishing.

"He is my friend . . . Uncle No Nose." Chai growl furiously and jab the nearest kite boy on the face and push at another forcefully. They know him and his family's reputation. Some shy aside to think twice, a few of them don't look satisfy, they move forward.

Chai stand by to fight.

"Chai . . ." Yeow sweep on his chest with his sliced hand, swift and light. "Not their fault . . ." And just baby-smiles at kite boys exchanging glance with No Nose.

No Nose jerk his head at kite boys. They break away to lean against the rope railings to watch. And then automatically No Nose blazing eyes change like cold steel. "Chai!" he call out with a pull of the kite line. Chai look at him. The point on the center of their eyes meet. Chai was hypnotize.

"Hold the oval tin," No Nose command.

Chai hold the oval tin.

"Coil it."

Chai coil the line while No Nose bring down the kite like nobody business, pulling down the line in long strokes with his typical black Chinaman farmer jacket, unbutton, revealing two dragons tattooed on his bony chest. And look at Yeow.

Yeow start to feel giddy, feel his whole body getting icy, he suck his own bloodied hand to feel pain for sensation and control, like gasping for breath. As he sucks, he gaze at No Nose.

No Nose was drawn to gaze back, he saw the image of a killer creature jump out of Yeow, lunge at him. Like guarding angel or whatever from the unexplains.

No Nose twist sideways to avoid direct contact and quickly dip into his big pocket jacket for a tin of tobacco and pass it to Yeow. "Na! Use it to stop the blood first . . . is only a scratch . . . ! You are lucky . . . ! I didn't slice your throat like a chicken. Come and visit me any time you like."

Yeow look tired. He took the tobacco halfheartedly and said, "Regardless, I will come and scratch your back. Time and place?"

"This place! No time . . . !" No Nose point at his own feet forcefully. "A thief can smell a thief better than a detective." And return to test his kite like nothing has happen.

Yeow felt a thief sage has awaken him. He took the tobacco and stop the bleeding. He nod a nice gesture at the punched boy and throw the empty tin to him. Punched boy catch it like it was a prize.

Down the bridge, on the road into Ho Swee village, Chai said, "Can you ride? Two more miles to go."

"Of course I can . . . !" Yeow frown with a disturb mind. "No, we walk, I like to walk, walk more see more," he insist and was quiet all the way, trying to work out No Nose privately.

He finally said, "Chai, do you know what happen to my hand, here?" Pressing the wounded hand against the wounded chin.

"Of course," Chai reply. "You have a scrap with my distant grand-uncle and the kite boys. I thought is all settle already. You still not satisfy?"

"What do you mean, your distant grand-uncle?"

"Ya," Chai nod his big head. "On my grandmother side, why?"

Yeow pause and said, "Do you remember you punch a kite boy and push at another . . . and coiling down the kite?"

"Kite? What kite . . . ?" Chai frown his brain and exclaim, "That No Nose must have hypnotize me!"

"Hypnotizing . . . ?"

"Yes, everybody in the village knows he can do it."

"You know any other thing about him?"

"No, not much . . . I don't even talk much with my old man. A lot of people in our village said he was a thief many years ago, long time ago," Chai said as they shortcut into wide and narrow lanes through the backyards, wells, kitchens, or toilets, and come out of the maze again into the main road created by the footsteps of war refugees running into Ho Swee Hill years ago.

Yeow keep the No Nose puzzles behind his head. His photographic mind keep snapping at the slum scene which amuse him, sometimes smiling at naked children squatting to shit as they tickle a pig sun-baking in a muddy pool beside them, grimacing at another pig eating up their scatter lumps of shits here and there. He ask casually, "So you and that shark-head boy split up because of spider business, right?"

"Ya . . . !" Chai lift up his faint brows and add, "My old man and his crazy Kung Fu father were on the same boat from China when they were about my age. Long time ago."

They approach the heart of the village at the intersection of the main road, a semi-marketplace of people gossiping among squeaky childrens playing free and wild.

"No street kids?" Yeow tease for more information.

"No, all are country pigs, some of them haven't seen the town yet, especially the girls."

"Nice?"

"Hard to find, nobody know how to dress properly."

"Not like us, haaa?" The tourist break out a charismatic smile.

"Don't know how to make money," Chai said amidst the busy center with more people stealing glance at Yeow's bloodstain white shirt and leather shoes.

"Chai, I am starting to feel ticklish. . . . Too many eyes swimming at me."

"That is nothing, they always like that at outsiders. There . . . !" Chai points toward the playground. "That the place all the spider boys play. My house is the big one behind that very old banyan tree."

Yeow caught the sight of Kim with a few girls fleeting glances at him as they cross the road on the opposite direction. "Hey, Chai," he whisper and wink. "Who is that girl with the short skirt and a big T-shirt without a bra, red handkerchief around her ponytail . . . ? The chicken-leg one, you saw?" And smile.

Although Chai's head is big, his eyes is quick and sharp like his grandmother Ah Paw. "Don't talk, saw everything . . . !" he said. "That one walk in and out like husband and wife with that shark-head boy, they grow up in the same house together."

"She is tall like women, too much for him. How old?"

"A bit younger than him. About a year. Why? You fancy her . . . ?"

Yeow has never talk to anybody about girls. Chai's sudden remark make him shy. "No, no, no . . ." he said. "Let's not talk about girls, I go to your house for a wash first. Come again some other time. Today is not my day."

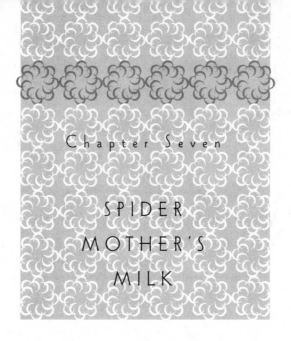

Chapter Seven

SPIDER
MOTHER'S
MILK

More months have passed. Spider fames for Kwang spread further to other corners of Singapore. He catch more spiders. Everywhere he go, he wins, his income and his followers multiply. His house without mother rule turn into community center for more spider boys hanging around to court friendship. Like those born during the Japanese occupation, he too was also growing taller into youthhood with a stronger image of his father. A temple has emerge on his throat to make his voice change. "Always wins!" he boast to Kim.

Weeks ago: He saw Kim washing clothings by the well in one burning hot afternoon when nobody is around. He wonder why and walk over to her after catching spiders. She splash a handful of water at him.

He took off his shirt and flip it over his shoulder and squat in front of her. "Frog legs . . . !" He rubs her bare leg and ask, "Want to go out and see picture at the Railways? Tarzan tonight." Glancing at her underpants barely cover by her shortening skirt as she grow, and stares in a startle. "Hey . . . ! What? What happen down there . . . !"

She squeeze her thighs together with her always ready to laugh eyes, dead looking. "I don't know why," she look down quietly. "I have blood coming out, here." And open her legs.

He look around, there was nobody there. He pick up a piece of her underwear from the bucket to examine it. "Hey, more blood here! Why?" He tighten up his tight face.

Kim bend her head down to soaps and scrubs a dirty panty against the washing board up and down without a word for a while before she said, "Don't know what happen . . . it come and go a few months ago."

"Painful?"

"No . . ."

"Anybody know . . . !"

"No, nobody know—don't want anybody to know for nothing and make big story. Can you take me to see a doctor in town?" She looks down to scrub the washing aimlessly.

"Of course . . . !" he bigger his small eyes. "I take you today . . . don't worry . . . ! Worry is the worst thing . . . !" In a gripping voice with vein showing up on his throat.

"Don't talk so loud . . . !" she shout quietly with a sprinkle of water on his face. "You go inside and wait for me." Follow by a smile as she stares into the tunnel of his quick pupil.

And he went straight into her bedroom in the steaming hot afternoon. And walks up and down to wait. While Ah Seow was still at school and his little brother were playing a mile away at the playground by the old banyan tree.

The moment she steps in, she said, "Is like that." As she push aside the mosquito net to sit on the edge of her bed. "I just had a bath and wash away the sticky blood." Lifting her legs to strip down her underpants reluctantly, unsure of herself by a moment, and yet doing it in slow motion with naughty looks at his fix eyes, giggles a little at him.

He watch her like spiders in action, watch her kick away her underwear, one leg down with thighs greasing apart to reveal a faint patch of black hairs sprouting round her vagina. She edge forward on her bed a little, and splitting her legs farther apart again.

"You can look now," she say meekly.

He touch her knee to bend down and squat in between her legs at the bed edge. Scanning at her vagina with a scratch of his head. "Last time you don't have curly hairs there." He touch her curly patches with a fingertip skating backward and forward lightly.

"Last time . . . what?" she ask in a carry-away type of voice.

"Last time, last time . . . when we didn't wear underpant . . . !" he recall. "When our mother nearly killed us for copying Panther Tiger cocking, your father nearly fight with your mother—you remember?"

"You make me do it . . . !" She tighten her full lips. "I am scare now"—with a quiver—"don't touch me like that." She heave a breath and grips her legs together with both hands pressing his hand tightly inside her thighs. "Our mother will beat us to death." And jerk a shiver as her heart beat faster, feeling the lashing whip of past inflicted by her mother mix together with burning lust to dare again.

A magic moment set her body ablaze. She wriggles her bottom with her hands smoothing the cane scars on his body. The tension of his lean hard body harden up like refusing to surrender to pain. She felt it as she caress his shoulder and nibble at it.

"Panther Tiger bites," she heave a whisper. "You like leather and never scare."

She was right. He was bold and leather. He pull down his short shorts. "You want to see mine? I also have some hairs around here too now." And his prick spring up with a throttle.

Nature spark sensation over the carefree and wild naive tomboy reputed to be the most beautiful flower of the village by all matchmakers. They say, "She is perfectly proportion. Her eyes can fish down the moon."

Her body vibrates up and snaps the chains of fear. They ride each other like sex-hungry wrestling spiders again and again, with more pleasure after a break of about five years or so. Sweating under atap roof inside her mosquito net curtained messily around her blooded bed. Slumbering together until Kwang's little brothers came back from play to demand money for food.

Then he took her to town for a checkup.

Inside the clinic, the kind old doctor said, "Don't worry, is very natural. From now on you will be having your periods every months until you have a baby or getting old like me. You are a very beautiful girl. Don't let anybody cheat you."

They don't give a damn. They make more love, they share everything! She cooks for his little brothers. Even insist on helping to wash their clothings with fresh energy. They go to market together, they eat together day and nights. Kwang feel brand-new. Even the scars of stress on his face accumulated from his mother's rule evaporates. He start to look sparkling. He took her out to see the colors and variety of Chinatown by night, bought clothings and eat foods cook in front of them in a flaming wok. It dazzle Kim who didn't leave the village all her life. She love it and was very happy. Happy make her more beautiful as she continue to grow.

One early morning, at their usual place by the big yam leaves, Ah Seow said, "Money always rolling in, people come to us. Everybody said you can win the big one this year. Do you know that?" To lift his boss higher.

"Not so easy." Kwang yawns and open a box for a Mr. Spider to come out and jump between his hands.

"I also think you can," Ah Seow poke about. "Another six months for you to become this year new king of spider boys." And squat down to sort out the spider boxes.

"No need you to tell me, lah ... aaah ... !" He grumble and wave away Ah Seow's curious goodwill in a sudden change of temperament, turn round to let his spider leap into a big yam leaf to relax and enjoy morning dew. Watching dreamily with Kim on his mind privately.

The more he watch his spiders on the leaf, the more he think of Kim with odd thoughts in his creative mind. Wondering about what will happen to his spiders if Kim allow them to drink her period blood. "My spiders ..." he ponder. "Live on my blood from my bedbugs. Kim is fierce. Maybe my spiders likes her blood too? Maybe should try out few and see what happen first?"

When his best spider has finished drinking and walk about on the big leaf, he let out a female spider to make love and watch them under his magnifying glass.

Ah Seow who watch his strange behavior hiddenly didn't say much all morning. On the way down from the farmer's plot, he ask, "Do you know Yeow came to our village with Chai a few days ago?"

"Who told you?"

"San . . . !"

"What he say?"

"Nothing much . . . San just say Chai's luck is bad. You should ask the kite boys, they are all laughing about it."

"Did he stay long?"

"I think . . . no." Seow shakes his head. "San didn't say. . . . I think he just come and smell around about you, or Chai showing off. What you think?"

"Showing off," the boss answer at once with a wave.

"You scare of Chinatown Yeow?" Ah Seow start to poke around.

"Scare what!" Kwang bark. "You just said things anyhow. He dare to come to our place, I dare to go to his place. I am going to Chinatown today. You want to come with me?"

"No, not free," the brainy coward said. "I have a lot of school homework to do." Walking faster as the slopes get steeper.

The same morning Kwang skip school and said to Kim on the way to eat at the village market, "I going out to buy you cotton for your blood—still a lot coming out this time?"

"Same as yesterday. Where you going? Chinatown?"

"Yah, you want to come?"

"What time coming back?"

"Up to you." He shrug his shoulder with open hands.

"Daytime is no fun, go at night." She hold his hand and they walk.

He swings her hand and said, "I think of you this morning when I was watching my spiders drinking . . ."

"About what?" She stop swinging hands, smilely.

"About my spiders drinking your that blood and see how."

"What? What you think I am . . . ?" She slap his face. "Your spider's mother milk?"

"Don't be like that." He rubs his face. "You always say we can always talk anything together, remember?"

"Go away!" She push him away.

"Don't be like that . . . !" He lie, "I just joking."

She flatten her full lips at him. "You think until there is nothing to think and still thinks!" With a frame of mind laughing inside, enjoying an itchy exotic feeling with spiders drinking from her vagina. The more she play around with her thoughts, the more she want sex.

They make love again when Ah Seow went to school in the afternoon. Giggling at a male spider drinking a drop of her blood when she squat over the spider box.

"I let a female hop in, see what happen?" he ask and let her jump in. She jump in, male go for her in a frenzy and make love on the spider box under Kim's vagina in a crumble.

Kim get more excited, a large drop of her period blood land on top of both spiders. Spiders don't care until it was too late when the blood dried and cement them together and died.

They both feel bad.

From then on they stop making love. Kim has vomiting feelings about dead spiders inside her every time they try.

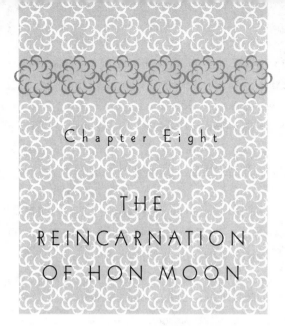

Chapter Eight

THE REINCARNATION OF HON MOON

The busy South Bridge Road through Chinatown runs parallel to a long stinking monsoon canal flowing into the Singapore River. Over the canal is a concrete bridge with the Nam Tain Cinema on one end and a popular bus stop on the other. During rush hours, ladies usually pull out their change from their purse before they go into the squeezy bus in a hurry. Sometimes coins roll down into the canal. Under the bridge has a concrete stairs where rejected street kids of Yeow goes down the canal to search for lost coins and salvage rubbish for recycling at peak hours, trying to make their own living when the day cools down. Sometimes tourists throw coins for them to scramble in the stinking sludge and take photo.

On the bridge. Yeow has a habit of relaxing against the railings to watch life go by at sunset time when street hawkers' activities start to dress up Chinatown. It gives him depths and inspire his visions and ambitions. That day, that time, he was watching stubborn Sachee who start to rebel, waddling breast deep among a dozen bigger boys in the stenchy canal, sinking his rattan shovel like a half wok into the black sludge, shaking the black water to wash out for coins, saving tin cans and metal scraps to one side on the canal stairs with Big Mole squatting beside his finds.

Kwang and Kim happen to have just finished watching a movie at the Nam Tain. They drink sugarcane water outside the cinema. And cross the busy bridge.

"Hey, that is Chinatown Yeow. . . ." Kwang stop and point to Kim and walk forward.

"What is so big about him?" She pull Kwang backward by the collar with her long hand. And peer over his head to look at Yeow leaning on the bridge railing watching down the canal.

"See if he has anything to say." Kwang walk faster forward. "Yeow!" he yell out at a few meters away.

Yeow swung around. "Hey . . . ! What are you doing here? Almost can't recognize you, you taller a lot . . . !" Surprisingly, with a very welcome face.

"Just came out of Nam Tain," Kwang grin back delightly.

"Aah . . . ?" Yeow lift his smooth brows at Kim. "*The Living Desert*, all about animals in the hot sand. I saw it twice."

Kim tips a glance at him and shy away to watch the boys in the canal.

Yeow second glance at her and said to Kwang, "Are you all together?" Pointing between them.

"Yah, this is Kim." Kwang rubs her slim waist and introduce her with a thumb. "Kim, Yeow."

Kim turn around. Yeow nod and baby-smile. "Good movie?"

Country girls always feel inferiority complex in town. Kim is no different. The handsome and well-dress Yeow make her feel uncomfortable. "Not bad," she snubs quietly and return to look at the boys slogging in the canal.

"I think I saw her once when I came to your village with Chai some time ago," Yeow smile at Kwang.

"Really?" Kwang dance his small eyes bigger. "I heard from somebody you came. For what?" he grin.

One was smiling. One was grinning. Both were sparkling.

"Just looking. What about you now—going home?"

"No, look around first." Kwang pats his girlfriend's back. "Kim, want to walk now?" With a wink at Yeow.

Yeow thumb-up at him and wink behind her back. She saw it as she turn to go around. Their eyes engage a moment.

"This means you," Yeow thumb-up at her. "Very beautiful—don't look so angry."

"You know how to talk," Kim smile up. "Why you here?"

"Watch them," Yeow point and shout down the canal with hand around the mouth. "Sachee! You have had enough!"

Sachee look up with his mudded black face and don't care. He waddle his way stubbornly toward Big Mole on the canal's stairway with a handful of electrical wires for burnt down into copper. Big Mole whisper aloud fast, "He is calling you! Better go up quick!"

Sachee slam his rattan shovel against the canal stairway. "No!" he grunt.

"Everybody come up!" Yeow hail a louder shout.

All the rebellious canal boys scramble up the stairs.

"Sachee," Big Mole shakes his arm, "better go up now . . . !"

"No . . . !" Sachee shakes his head with a splash of his hands on the stenchy water below the stairway.

"Make any eats?" Yeow ask the first boy who climb up.

"Only scraps, Sachee pick up a few coins," the boy said and bash his rattan shovel against the side railing of the bridge for the dirts to rain into the canal.

Another boy with shorts dripping wet, swing down his wet sack from his naked shoulder. "Yeow," he ask timidly. "Any loopholes for a job?"

Yeow open a hand in front of all the boys around him and gesture at Kwang proudly. "Meet my friend Kwang, from Ho Swee Hill, and his girlfriend . . . er . . . Kim." Hastily after remembering her name with a breaking smile.

All those boys crowd around to shake their dirty hands with them enviously like they were VIPs. A few of them says to Kwang, "We have clash spiders before." One of them said, "I heard a lot about you." Another one said, "I remember you fighting at Nam Tain Lane with one of us."

Kwang's head swell, his ears turn red. "Come to my place!" he invite them with sparkling face.

Yeow sip a smile confidently, like a man born to rule. Kim snub a lousy look at his commanding confidence and shake Kwang's shoulder. "Don't talk so much. I want to go now."

Yeow's super sense seldom miss anything. He knew she feel left out among all the boys. "Can you wait?" he said to her. "I go down to get Big Mole and Sachee up first." When he walk down the slippery canal stairway with his smart clothings his boys stand in awe.

"Sachee, Sachee . . . !" Big Mole bites her fingernail. "He is coming down to get us, better go up fast . . . !"

"So what . . . !" Sachee growl. "He touch me again, I bite him!"

Yeow pull his neat trouser over the knees to squat beside Big Mole. And taps at the back of Sachee's muddy shoulder. "Hey, big man," he ask quietly. "Want to come with me? That shark-head boy call Monkey Boy you always talk about is up there, I am eating together with him. Big Mole, you coming?" And walk up.

Big Mole scratches her fuzzy hair. "Yeow will be very mad! I am going up. You want to come?" Lifting up a jute sack with some of Sachee's finds inside.

Sachee knows his time is up. He follows Big Mole.

The sun sets. The day cools down. Road lights on the main road appear on lampposts. The jovial party mingle along as the bright lights of Chinatown start to light up. More people come and go. Afternoon school for children dismisses, night classes for adults get ready, traffic starts to jam. The Majestic, Kim Wah, Nam Tain, Tong Hong cinemas start to flash their neon signs for another show. Evening markets begin. Hawkers of all kinds pump up their powerful kerosene lamps in all directions on the pavement of roads and streets to lift up Chinatown with more variety and color and competition and people. Bargains getting louder and louder. The momentum of gaiety increases.

In good mood, everybody was high. Those canal boys isolated by Yeow feel like they were walking back to happiness. Kwang and Kim are like stars among them. Kwang was their new hero, especially to Sachee who knew he was Chai's rival. Chai has threatened to beat him up ever since he let down his tires. Kim is scare of traffic, makes everybody laugh when she hesitates about as they cross busy roads.

Big Mole was happy to lead her across. Big Mole ask with her brown Malay face, "Where do you stay?"

"Ho Swee Hill, you know where?" Kim ask back.

"Don't know where," Big Mole say.

"Any job for me there?" Sachee join in loudly.

"Plenty of job to carry shits . . . !" Yeow tease.

"Just asking also cannot!" Sachee throw out a fist.

"The moon is bright tonight, come tonight?" Kim tugs Big Mole's scrawny hand. "Late night at our temple tonight . . . !"

"Ask Yeow first," Big Mole whisper meekly.

Kim tap on the back of Yeow with hands on hips. "Bossy Face, do I have to ask you for her to my house?"

Yeow flip a thumb sideways at her boyfriend. "Ask him."

"Don't have to ask him," she snap back at Yeow and turn to Big Mole. "You come tonight. . . . What is your name?"

"Everybody call me Big Mole," she said sadly.

Kim feel terrible for her. "Kwang . . . !" she demand with a slap on his shoulder. "Big Mole is coming. I want to buy something now and cook at home."

All the canal boys turn heads at embarrass Kwang. He feel lost face, ignores her.

Nothing escapes ambitious Yeow, a concrete dreamer who read people for his ambition surefootedly day by day. He mini-smile and arms round Kwang to whisper in his ears, "Don't worry about lost face with my boys, you better please Kim. If she is not your girlfriend I will chase after her."

"That means very give face," gentleman Kwang whisper back. "If she likes you, is okay by me. Just don't play dirty." With a serious face that means what he say.

Yeow was shock and touch too. Nobody so much younger than him has ever dare to challenge him so directly since he was nickname China-town Yeow. Sixth sense told him at once that Kwang was a good find. "Don't worry about me on a girl," he assure him quickly and turn around. "Big Mole, go with Sachee if you can find a place to sleep. I come and see you all tomorrow."

"Big Mole," Kim says carefreely, "you and Sachee sleeps at Kwang's mother's bedroom. Kwang can sleep back at his old room with his small brothers."

Moving on. They follow the canal boys into back lanes with old prostitutes and opium smokers shadow in and out of back doors. And out into Kalangori Lane where old men living in tents buys and sells scraps from old clothing to rags for wiping mechanics' oily hands, old newspapers to duck feathers, anything that can be recycle. Canal boys sell what they have to sell and give their sacks and shovels back to the Kalangori men.

Out of Kalangori Lane. They came on the outskirts of Chinatown to Neil Road, where a woman in her fifties has a cigarette stall on the doorsteps of her house in a row of prewar one-story houses. Canal boys troop in like soldiers returning to their barrack after hard labor. They are not the working type, but will fight at the snap of Yeow's finger for three meals, sometimes some pocket money.

"Ah Soh," Yeow ask the cigarette woman. "Anybody looking for me?"

"Only Chai, he said is not important," the cigarette woman reply and look at Kim and Kwang. "Have you all eaten yet? Where do you all come from?" Motherly.

Both of them don't like mothers and be treated like kids, felt uneasy. Kim look at Kwang, Kwang didn't bother to answer, instead he said, "Yeow, we make a move first. We have a cup of coffee together some other times." Hand in hand with Kim.

"Alright, okay," Yeow smile. "I come and see you tomorrow."

After the four took off, Yeow squat next to the cigarette woman who sits on a rattan chair by her stall that also sells sweets and "eat bits" in jars. She roll up a cigarette and light it with the small kerosene lamp. "I like him," she said with a puff. "A lot of substance in that boy. Is he the one you talk about?"

"Yes." Yeow squints his eyes into empty space.

"What about that beautiful girl . . . ?"

"Grow up together in the same house."

"A pair of yin yang, a dazzling flower on a patch of cowdung," she comment. "Find out more about him first, bring him around for Cheong Pak to have another eyes on him. To rebuild Hon Moon you must have patience. Ten years is only a blink."

Together with her husband, Cheong Pak, they are caretakers of several houses bought by Yeow under their names. Cheong Pak was the financial adviser of the Hon Moon secret society, which has its roots in China but is extinguished when China turn red under Mao Tse-tung. The real insight of Chinatown is at the back of their hands. Yeow jointly owns all the picture comic rental stalls in Chinatown with Cheong Pak and his wife, who have no children of their own. His newspaper boys grown out of street kids run the distribution network in Chinatown. Almost all the coffee shop boys get their jobs through Yeow, because he can guarantee honesty for his boys who deals with cash. They become his ears.

Under Cheong Pak's management and advice, Yeow's business has grow until he don't know how much money he has. They also run a financial system called Wei that helps the hawkers of Chinatown pool their money together, to raise capital through bidding among members. Cheong Pak has said to Yeow, "Money glitters forever and holds the final cards. Societies are made of big and small gangs of all kinds, the government is a gang, your friend is your gang. Secret societies nowadays are full of headless gangs. They have the wrong guts and no set morals. That is why political gangs win in the end.

"Animal die for food. Man die for money. Our business must be spiritually and economically sound. Two sounds. In the end, business is about the spirit of cooperation. Those who cannot understand the virtues and strength of cooperation will never grow further. Don't forget that. Rub shoulder with the brilliants will give you brilliance. I have learn my lessons."

Yeow, who seldom smoke, took a menthol cigarette from a tin which sells by the sticks separately. Smokes with teeth biting the filter and said to the cigarette woman, "I will be going to Ho Swee Hill tomorrow like you and Cheong Pak says. Spend more time there. . . . I am thinking of finding a place there too. If that Shark Head can bend all the spider boys away from Chai he can easily lead all my boys in Chinatown—with him maybe taking the crown of spider boys this year, hmmm . . . ?" He smile.

"Very soon you will have an army of Impossibles," she say with her roll-up between finger. "When are you going back to Penang and bring back your auntie's bones?"

"I will tell you when I am ready."

"Pull the hands of Kwang and Chai together first," she advise before Yeow walk away.

Yeow eat at his favorite Ho San coffee shop by the picture comic rental stall. He stroll toward Santeng with Kim and Kwang rubbing his mind. At Santeng's busy foothill, he change his mind and decide to go to Ho Swee Hill for a surprise visit. He catch a taxi to the mouth of Ho Swee Hill with a torchlight.

Unlike Chinatown which awakes by night, Ho Swee village sleeps by night and wake up early. Is silence by night, especially at the outskirt. The contrast atmosphere of peace and tranquillity suit him fine.

At the rickety No Nose Bridge, he leans on the railings to look at the Ho Swee River under the reflection of the pearly moon that carpets her silver lining on the black water and give him romance, make him lonely. It makes emotions go up and down. Lone wolf inside howling.

When somebody walk on the creaky bridge, the whole bridge moves. He saw a figure pushing a bicycle with headlights shining, he suddenly wish that was Chai, and it was.

"Hey! Yeow!" Chai blast out. He push his bike faster. "How come you are here? I look for you everywhere!"

"Blown by the winds tonight," Yeow said as they walk.

"You talking strange," Chai said. "What winds?"

"Coincidence," he said in his usual quiet manner. "How is saltish luck? Ah Soh said you looking for me."

"Nothing much, luck's good. . . . Are you coming to the village to look for me?" Chai guess delightly.

"I meet Kwang and Kim at Nam Tain Bridge today—Big Mole and Sachee is staying with them tonight."

"What . . . ! Sachee also there!" Chai pounds his bike handle. "I don't feel comfortable with that little rat around!"

"Sachee is only a small boy. . . . Don't make small matters mount on him." He pacify with a pat on Chai's beefy shoulder. "Give me a lift."

Chai shakes his head down with nothing to say and give him a lift below No Nose Bridge under full moon night.

As Chai peddles, Yeow said, "I want to find a place to stay in this village. You jack it up for me?"

"No problem. I ask San to ask his father. He knows the village like that," Chai flips his hand left and right. "When?"

"Any time. . . . I stay at your place tonight?"

"Sure," Chai says and bikes.

For the past few months Chai's friendship with Yeow has grown like brothers, he has learn to accept that Yeow is always right. The way Yeow throw money around make his spider business look small. The wrangles with Kwang has come to a point where he has to start to accept defeat and lost his sense of direction. His telltale clock at nearly fifteen years old also signal the time to retire from childhood toys of spider glory and money, he knew it.

Yeow said, "Money is easy to make. People are hard to find."

"What kind of people you want?" Chai ask.

"People with brains and nerve in the guts, like you and Kwang join together to run my street boys business."

"How much will you pay me? Friendship is another thing, we talk straight first."

"Good," Yeow said. "Straightforward between you and me is best, I will pay you three hundred dollars a month."

"What? Three hundred dollars...! That is more than five times I make in a month! I make more than a man make in this village. What I do...?"

"Just round up my boys and see they don't fight each other and steal things around in Chinatown."

"So easy? When...!"

"Not easy. When you and Kwang become friends again."

The changing smell of incense and joss sticks burning at the Kuan Yin Temple's late night for full moon. People gossip like shadows in a village grown out of old burial ground. Looks spooky to outsider Yeow who has just emerged out of a quiet biking night. Rubbish was burning in scatter patches by children having a good time around the fires at the playground by the old banyan.

Yeow starts to talk. "Chai, I can smell it.... This place is like San-teng, full of old bones who know a lot."

His world is too abstract for Chai most of the time—Chai doesn't bother about it. "Over there...!" Chai point ahead. "Can you see? That Shark Head and his boys is over there under the big beard tree."

"Good one, see how he act." Yeow muse and ask, "Chai, you come with me?"

Chai light up a smoke and shakes his head. "No. no, you go yourself. I wait for you in front of my place."

"Come on," Yeow insist. "Grow up a little bit more and make small problem disappear. What is there to lose face? Is good for all of us . . . !"

Chai didn't argue and went along reluctantly.

It didn't take long for Kwang's boys to spot them. They report to Kwang.

"Chinatown Yeow here . . . ?" Ah Seow the hero worshiper ask in excitement.

"Spread the news," Kwang said at once. "Tell all our people to come here, I introduce Chinatown Yeow to them."

"That's the way . . . ! Show them our numbers!" Ah Seow sells to make them rush away like winds.

Those winds hit Yeow with surprise. "Hey? Why they flock away . . . ?" Watching the lone figure of Kwang stood up to walk toward them with Ah Seow following.

"They will come back to show off their numbers." Chai grumbles. "I lost a lot of them to him . . . !"

As they approach, Ah Seow ask his boss, "Do you know why he is coming with Chai here tonight?"

Kwang didn't reply, but was anticipating the same question. "If I want something, I go to him. He want something? He come to me. Wait and see is the best," he concluded.

"Come to see you for a change," Yeow smile with his telltale eyes between Kwang and Chai who shy away from each other to look groundward. He stretch his hand over at Ah Seow to break the ice by catching the smaller fly first. "I am Yeow," he introduce himself.

Ah Seow jump his hand to shake Yeow's friendly hand. "I am Seng!" he tremble nervously at the famous name.

"People here call him Ah Seow," Chai join in. "Ah Seow . . . !" he ask. "Have you seen San?"

"I see him walk past with a bottle to catch fireflies just now, going uphill," Kwang answer to make Chai feel easy.

Yeow steal the occasion and turn to Ah Seow. "Seng," he said. "Why not find a place to wait around here first?"

Overwhelm by Yeow's attention and called Seng instead of a crazy nickname all the time, "Okay, okay," Ah Seow reply fast and led the way.

Leaving Kwang and Chai behind them. "Seng," Yeow measure a hand above the ground. "Have you seen a nuggety boy with a chubby face this tall . . . and a skinny girl about your height with a big mole under the eye?"

"I know, I know," Ah Seow repeat in a hurry. "They go out with my sister to visit her friends."

"Kim your sister?" Yeow exclaim quietly with a finger and start to ex-change conversation with Ah Seow.

Following behind slowly, Kwang start to feel sorry and puzzle by the way Chai looks and follows Yeow. He place a hand on his bicycle as they walk. "How is luck outside? I might be going to Pasir Panjang to test that area out in a day or two. Maybe we should join force and have a look. Want to come?" His head turn to Chai.

Chai bite a thought. "Why go so far?"

"There is nothing much happening around."

"I have been even further—up to Changi! Everywhere is the same at this time. Wait for the kite season to finish in another month and then it will pick up." And their friendship was united like old time again.

Kwang shut up as they join the gathering of spider boys crowding around Ah Seow's new hero. When they arrived, all the spider boys stood up to make way for their reunion. And they all cherish the night with Yeow rubbing his hands quietly inside.

Chapter Nine

BIG
SPIDER

When the hands of
Kwang and Chai was pull together, Yeow rent a
house in the village for Big Mole and Sachee to
live. Big Mole and Kim became close friends.
Chinatown is not new to Kim anymore. Sometimes Kwang stay out for a day, then a few days,
and give up schooling without his mother
knowing about it. Wrestling spider matching
inside the village have dulled down without
major matches between Kwang and Chai.

One Saturday afternoon the rain was drizzling on and off. On the bamboo deck of the

house with no parent rule, Big Mole was laying upward on the deck, watching a wall lizard on the atap roof catching mosquitoes, said driftily, "I wish I had a lot of money."

Kim replaiting a pigtail, tease, "Like you should marry a rich man, become second wife also never mind—is that right?"

"Third wife also never mind," Big Mole reply. "But I am ugly, nobody want me—you see?" Pointing at her big mole.

"Money also cannot make your mole disappear," Kim said bluntly. "What you do with money? Tell me first."

"Why you so stupid?" Big Mole said. "Money can do anything."

Sachee the little spy, teaching a new game of cards to Kwang's two little brothers and other boys their age, throws down his card. "I like fighting fish . . . ! Start a fighting fish shop!" Scrambling to join Big Mole.

"Sachee is right . . . !" Big Mole sits up. "Maybe we can breed pet fishes ourself. Anybody breeding pet fish in this village? No need big capitals."

"No, nobody . . . !" Ah Seow answer as he feed Kwang's spiders with bedbugs on the round table.

"Ask your boss to talk to Yeow," Big Mole said with a sudden healthy look shining out from her normal dull face of hopelessness and aimlessness.

"Better talk to Chai first," Ah Seow advise. "Chai can smell money. If he agree, Yeow will agree."

"Don't talk to Chai . . . !" Sachee shake his fist at Seow. "If he knows, nothing will be left for us . . . ! The most is only bones!"

"Big man . . . ! You talk so big," Kim turn around at Sachee. "How many kinds of fish you want to breed?"

"Only fighting fish," Sachee insist.

"All kinds, any kinds that sells," Big Mole answer.

Ah Seow ask, "How are you going to feed them?"

"Mosquito larvae . . . ! Plenty around!" Sachee cries out.

"Ya . . . ! Mosquito larvae!" Big Mole exclaim and fold Sachee around her. "We know a lot of things you all don't know."

Kim challenge her impulsively. "What you get for doing it? It is still not your business."

Unlike impulsive fiery Kim, Big Mole is more deep, she mumbles quietly, "I want to have my own money—become rich one day for everybody to see." Boiling with emotions beneath her own reasons, about to burst out tears, and yet holding herself together with a certain kind of toughness season from being the only gang girl in Singapore. She cuddles Sachee tighter.

"Don't let Chai know," Sachee warn like top secrets.

"Why . . . !" Kim stretch a long leg to tickle his chubby body.

Offended at not being treated like an equal, he grab her leg with a push forward and yell, "Don't look small on me!" Surprisingly fast and strong, sending her falling backward.

Rubbing her bumped head, she comes back to tickles him harder to annoy him more. "Why, why . . . ? Why?"

Knowing he can't win, he plead playfully, "Don't be like that, lah . . . ! I don't like to fight with girl."

"Sachee," Big Mole pushes him off her lap. "Go back and play your card, I talk to you later."

Sachee took off. Ah Seow went back to his room to study. Leaving the girls alone to do their girl talk. Big Mole was on his mind. Ah Seow likes her curly Arabic eyes and brown smooth skin. In his room, he can hear them talking.

"Want to see a movie tonight?" Kim's voice.

"I don't have money like you." Big Mole's voice.

"Don't talk like that, I shout you."

"You shout me all the time—no, I don't feel like going anywhere."

"Why you so moody today?"

"Talk out also no use, you cannot help."

"About fish business?"

"Lots more than that—how old do you think I am?"

"About my age, maybe more. Nearly thirteen? Fourteen? Why?"

"I—I don't even know my age," Big Mole sniff a sob. "I have no name . . . I am not Chinese . . . I am not sure. . . ."

"Don't cried, cried also no use. Where do you come from? Don't be scare to tell me, tell me everything."

The girls' voices get softer and unclear. Ah Seow sneak into his parents' room with wall against the deck to peep through a gap in the planks.

"Don't tell anybody, I have never tell anybody about myself before." Big Mole lift up her wraparound skirt to wipe her eyes. "I remember I live on prahu boat with my dog to many places." She draw aimlessly with a finger on the bamboo deck. "One time many people rush to our boat, my Papa scream, my dog stop barking. Mama carry me away and jump into the sea near the bank, crawl with me to the street with many people pushing and running, my Mama fell down—I was push away. I cannot see my Mama. . . ." She sniff and sobs more as she recollect her ordeal during the Japanese occupation.

Kim rubs her shoulder. "And then?"

"A woman found me, took me away, and I live with her. She is a prostitute. Sometimes she get crazy and beats me."

"So you run away?"

"Yes, three or four years ago," Big Mole manage a smile. "She sold me to another prostitute house in Kong Saik Road." And lie down with starey eyes up at the wall lizard on the atap roof.

Kim also ease herself. She lay down and nibbles the end of her pigtail to watch Big Mole. Sharing a silence moment together for a while. And said, "They prostitute you? You prostitute before you run away?"

"No, not old enough, slave girl. Bring a bucket of water into the room before the man go in, take the water out when he finish washing his stick after playing, clean up all the prostitute's dirty sponges in the wash room—"

"What dirty sponge!" Kim cut in with a startle.

"That is what prostitute used before they sleep with men."

"How? Dirty sponges?"

"The dirty sponges has the fucking man's juice—this size." She squeeze her palm into a tight fist. "Like that . . . to push it in their hole to stop the man juice make them sick inside, also not make babies." She squat and demonstrate few thrust under her wraparound with a peep at Kim's face poking closer.

Kim wriggles her shapely body and ask closely, "Have you seen them sleeping together?"

"Common for me—seen a lot."

Ah Seow's peeping and listening was blown up by the voice of Kwang limping up the three flight stairs. "Where is Ah Seow . . . ? Where is Ah Seow?" His body soaking wet by the drizzling rain.

Ah Seow frown and came out quickly. "What so big news?"

"Don't talk much first...!" Kwang beam the biggest grin Ah Seow has ever seen before. "I show you all something first." And open up a spider box with everybody crowding around. "This is the king!" he declare.

"Waah...! So big?" Ah Seow's eyes pop. "Let me have a bounce...!" Straightaway. And bounce the biggest wrestling spider he ever saw.

"This is the king," his boss gleam and block it back into his hand to box it up with a kiss on the box surface.

"Where—you—catch—it?" Ah Seow ask word by word.

"Same place."

"How you catch it?" Sachee cut in.

"Very strange." The boss swallow his mouth water. "I step on a rusty nail. I sit down and pull lalang grass to bandage the blood, then...! This king jump on my lap, jump off. So big, at first I thought was an insect...! So I don't care and bandage my leg again..."

"And then?" Sachee interrupt.

"And then it jumps on my lap again...! Lucky it didn't jump down, jump up...! Jump up to hide inside sandwich leaves. When I cup the leaves and caught it, I still don't believe it." He sit back contentedly with an aching pain on his face cause by the infections in the foot and wince. "Got headache, I want to sleep first." And limps into his room.

Big Mole push at Sachee. "Go and find him a stick to walk."

The next day, Kwang's leg get worse, more swollen, but he still limp about with the umbrella handle Sachee find him, to train his new spider. Lost his appetite to eat. At night, he cannot sleep, suffering from a high fever with a burning mind, talking in bad dreams, a lot to do with spiders and his mother.

The following morning before cock crow, the boss tosses about in bed with Kim fanning him with newspapers. "Hot, hot, very hot——!" he gasp. "Ah Seow, feed my king first . . . inside my pillow."

"This Panther Tiger is a devil. . . ." Kim said with a painful face, rubbing Tiger Balm on Kwang's forehead, nostril, throat, massaging his chest continuously not knowing exactly what to do.

"I go and ask Big Mole to come here first." Ah Seow ran off to wake up Big Mole and Sachee.

Just after cock crows, the trio rushes back.

"Very hot . . . !" Big Mole said with a shock and withdrew her hand on his forehead. "Sachee," she whisper. "Quick, find Yeow and ask Vegetable Auntie to help you buy some ginseng before you come back." She dig into her secondhand flowery samfoo top and pull out a plastic bundle with her life savings.

"Buy two dollars." She fish out the money. "Come back quickly——!"

The moment Sachee sped off, Ah Seow said to the girls, "I go and tell San's father first, he knows a lot."

After Ah Seow's report, in his office and living room combined, smoking Wong ponders up and down. "Aah——! Use Pung Tai Woon . . . !" he exclaim quietly and call out to his wife loudly, "Rice Woman! I am going out to save life! Tell my customers I am not free today!"

The clattering sound of sewing machine in the next room stop. "Are you coming back to eat?" San's mother shout back.

"Don't wait for me!" Wong reply and took out from his desk drawer a small metal box with opium hidden among some books and stacks of square red brushing paper. "Follow me," he said to Ah Seow with a wave befitting the ex–commander in chief of Hon Moon. And leads the way uphill to the weeds area for Pung Tai Woon that has edgy petal thumb size, also some Shameful grass which close itself with a touch.

"This is for his leg," he said with a fistful of Shameful Grass. "You come and pick some more tomorrow. If all this don't work—prepare to buy a coffin!"

News spread fast with Sachee around. When Wong and Ah Seow arrive, the house with no parent rule was full of spider boys. In Kwang's room, more of them pack up around him like mourners around a dying person. Wong has to usher them out to make space for fresh air.

"Very hot, hot, hot . . ." Kwang gasp and wriggles about with hands fighting to tear away his head. Kim and Big Mole trying to control his hands, two spider boys catch his kicking legs.

One look at him give Wong a shock. He pounds all the Pung Tai Woon in a granite pounder with one teaspoonful of salt, and squeeze the juice into Kwang's mouth. He rejects the bitter juice with shaky eyes and spew it out.

Soft tactics don't work. Wong shakes him repeatedly. "Look at me! Look at me!" he shout and smack his cheek rapidly. "Can you recognize me?"

Kwang nod his head dazedly with gasping tongue sticking out.

"Good!" Wong barks. "Drink it!"

Kwang drinks a little. Kim took the herb and squeeze it into his mouth as Wong laid him down. He drink more and more with starry eyes at Kim.

"Good ...!" Wong grin out his tobacco-color teeth at him. "Now close your eyeballs and breathe in and out slowly. I will put some on your head, your shark head will be alright in no time."

He paste the remaining herbs on his forehead, throat, and chest. The cooling cold Pung Tai Woon draws out the heat and turn warm. Make him drift away to sleep.

Wong shakes his head with relief and scan around the waiting faces of spider boys jam around the doorway of the room. And said warmly, "When he wake up, he will feel better. You all go home first and let him have a rest, come and see him tomorrow." They disperse quietly.

While Kwang was sleeping Wong look at his swollen leg and order for clean rags, hot water. Pounds up the Shameful Grass mixed with opium from his small box. And soak the sore foot inside a bucket with Shameful Grass as Kwang slumber.

"Watch him," he told Ah Seow. "Don't let him kick the bucket over when he move. If the water colds down ... let me know." He took off his glasses to massage his tired eyes and ask Kim, "Any coffee around?"

"Prepare already," Big Mole answer for Kim. "Waiting for you on the table outside."

"I have not seen you before." Wong straighten his glasses. "You look like a Malay girl."

"I am. . . ." Big Mole bites her fingernail shyly.

"Under the heaven. One family." Wong point a finger upward. And lead the way out to the bamboo deck for his coffee on the round table with Fatty's Family's cakes. He add opium into his black coffee and explain to the girls, "Pung Tai Woon must be drunk fresh with a few pinches of salt, should be able to drink in a bowl by himself when he wakes up. It is a very cooling herb, too much will make muscles in the leg weak. Half a bowl tonight, half a bowl in the morning, use what is left over to cover his forehead, throat, and chest." And chuckles. "Tomorrow he will spend the whole day visiting the toilet." He sips his black opiumed coffee.

Big Mole said, "I have ask Sachee to buy some ginseng."

"No, don't give ginseng to him yet . . . ! It is dangerous, it will clash. Both has cooling properties, it will upset the balance. Ginseng is good for increase vitality. Give it to him a week later."

"What about his leg? So swollen . . . !" Kim ask with painful expression on her face, as if it hurt herself.

"Heat inflames the poison infections," Wong said. "When his temperature cools down, the swelling will subside. The Shameful Grass works like magic, will draw out the remaining poison." He bite his cake. Watching space, high with thoughts, high by the opium in the coffee. Like want to be alone.

Big Mole drag Kim aside and whisper, "Don't forget to give that thick glasses man an angpow later. . . ."

"I am no good at all this motherly things—how much?"

"A dollar is alright, is for good luck too," Big Mole insist.

"Uncle Wong," Kim press the angpow into his hand. "A little bit of meaning." Shyly.

"Don't be stupid—!" Wong push it away. "I am closer to him than you, I owe his father my soul. To save a life is better than be a vegetarian a lifetime." And steps out of the bamboo deck.

Watching until lanky Wong stoop out of sight, Big Mole bites her fingernail thoughtfully. "Give him some opium for present. A present he don't know how to refuse."

In the early afternoon Sachee return with Yeow and Chai. They make him carry a big watermelon about half his nuggety size. He wobbles up the deck like a pregnant woman with two hands around the waist.

"Phew . . . ! Very heavy!" He dump it on the deck with a few dusty claps to make air at Chai.

"How is he?" Yeow ask in a hurry.

"Nearly die, lucky, San's father come and save him." Ah Seow talk fast and explain everything.

"Dead serious?" Chai ask Ah Seow with a quick glance at the girls. Big Mole turn her face the other way.

Kim nods slowly. "Yes, he scares me."

"Is he still sleeping?" Yeow point toward the room.

"Go inside and see him," Big Mole encourage meekly.

Yeow walk in at once. Everybody follows. Kwang curl up in a slumber clutching his spider box against his bosom peacefully. His lips is crack and dried. The straw mattress was messy with scatter bits of rag pieces, spill up herb pastes and juice marks. Smells of bitter herbs float in the air. Yeow draw in a few sniffs and wonder. "Can you smell opium?" he look at Chai.

Big-head Chai nose around and arrive at Kwang's foot. "Is here . . . !" he points at the bandage.

"Mr. Wong's recipe . . ." Big Mole twinkle a look at Yeow. "Kim give him an angpow, he refuse—maybe opium, to present him?"

Yeow smile and gesture Big Mole with his head to follow him out of the room. "Don't make noise," he said. "Keep your eyes open in China-town and here. . . . I am going to Penang for a week or two, maybe longer. Personal, don't ask."

The moment Ah Seow walk out, Chai tap at Ah Seow's shoulder and point at Kwang's spider box. "Big one there?"

Ah Seow finds it hard not to tell the truth at the facts, was excited about it. "Like that big," he gesture with a thumb.

And Sachee saw. The moment Yeow and Chai left, Sachee shakes his fist up at Ah Seow. "Don't let Chai know anything!"

Kim and Big Mole also give him the cheap look. Ah Seow walk off quietly with the insult for fresh air. Wondering, why? When he is right, nobody remember. When wrong, nobody forget. Took him quite a while to understand the power struggle between Chai, and Big Mole and Sachee, who found each other on common ground. "Chai . . ." he ponder. "Chai is not bad. . . . He is always hungry for money, but he is a gentleman, keeps his word. Even my sister is against me . . . ! Even dotty little Sachee thinks he can push me around!"

He questions. Questions and depression develop into anger. Anger develop into courage. Then he decided to go back and teach Sachee a lesson for barking at him.

He found Sachee eating the big watermelon with Kwang's brothers and a group of little boys. Mad with courage, Ah Seow went straight and twist his ear. "Next time don't try and act tough with me!"

Sachee eating a slice of watermelon with two hands, drops the wa-termelon and grab Ah Seow's ear, twisting hand. He sinks his teeth into Ah Seow's forearm. Ah Seow shakes and screams. The harder he shakes, the harder Sachee bite. He gnaw tighter and curl up like a ball to hang on Ah Seow's arm.

The screams brought Kim and Big Mole rushing out of the kitchen. One girl keep slapping Sachee's jaw, another tearing his clinching hands apart. Blood from Ah Seow's forearm was pouring all over the deck. Sachee's mouth was cover with blood, much redder than the watermelon juice around those small boys' lips and mouths watching the show, with Sachee as their new hero.

Humiliation in front of those watermelon faces make Ah Seow hot with rage. Sachee sense danger, he pick up the umbrella handle he found for Kwang. And stood his ground.

"You still want to fight . . . !"

"Go home! Go home!" Big Mole dash over and lead Sachee away. Ah Seow use the same Shameful Grass used on Kwang to heal Sachee's bite. News spread fast by the watermelon boys makes Ah Seow look more silly everywhere he go. Sachee turn into a greater hero with more small boys pack after him. When Kwang has fully recovered in less than a week, he too laugh about it.

From this day isolated Ah Seow becomes more independent. His friendship with Kwang that went through thick and thin together, begin to drift apart. San and him becomes closer friends. Taking Wong's advice, "It is much better to have brains than brawls," he pass his midterm examination with flying colors.

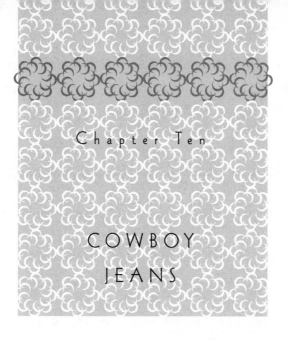

Chapter Ten

COWBOY
JEANS

Ambitious Yeow is also superstitious. He postponed his Penang trip to wait for the grave-visiting festival in the lunar month of May.

"Not a bad idea," the cigarette woman said, to encourage ancestor worship. "Your auntie's bones is our bones. Don't leave her alone in Penang for too long."

The day before leaving to get the bones back for reburial in Singapore, Yeow can't stop thinking about Old-timer, the Siew Jee Ho guy he killed for cheating him in Kuala Lumpur. It was a secret he kept only to himself. He quit his afternoon nap to look for Chai.

Chai was coming out of a small gambling den near the funeral parlors in Sago Lane in Chinatown.

"Chai . . . !" Yeow yell from behind. "How is luck?"

"Saltish luck," Chai mumble with his head shaking down. "Lost a few red ones again. . . ."

"You need this," Yeow toss him a packet of Lucky Strike. "Any problems around?"

"No, all under control. Not even small problems. You?"

"Going back to Penang to sort out a few things. . . . Come with me if you like, see a new world for a change."

"That is them give face, but who look out around here?"

"Good thinking," the boss flatters him. "You think for me."

Chai has no answers but he guess. "You scare of somebody there or what? If so, let me know. I rub them off for you."

"You think the wrong way," Yeow deny his hidden fear of the Siew Jee Ho. "Where is your bicycle?" he ask to sidetrack the situation of using Chai as bodyguard, indirectly.

"I lend it to Shark Head, you looking for him?"

"No, he is hard to catch. As long as you are all friends, I am happy. Okay?" He pats beefy Chai on the shoulder at the end of Sago Lane. And hails a trishaw for a slow ride to the Central Railway Station.

After sniffing around the busy place with bittersweet memories of his first landing in Singapore, Yeow book first-class on the Friday morning train. Feeling tense about the trip to Penang he buys a pair of dark glasses to disguise himself when he is there. Then looks at his

Rolex watch and decides to go fishing in a quiet shady spot under the Merdeka Bridge at the mouth of the Kallang River.

Fisherman of men, Yeow loves fishing. The echoes of splashing waves from the Java Sea under the biggest bridge of Singapore reflects his dream to climb the mountaintop. After a few more reflections he become clear of fear about going to Penang. "Fear not death, nothing to fear," he say inside himself and swing the line further, burnt a cigarette to wait. But still there was no bites.

He change side and immediately there was a sharp tug. It was a big-headed catfish with sharp spines behind its head and under the fins, that has venom like a stingray. It remind him of fearless Chai who live under his fat payroll. Yeow grab the spiky, vigorous fish by the tail and flung it back into the water. Chai has told all the Chinatown boys, "If anybody looking for trouble, fight with me first...!" and is effective. No trouble has break out yet.

As the tide gets higher the waves pound harder. He swings the line farther toward the Java Sea. Burnt another cigarette to ponder about Kwang getting more popular in every spider corners of Singapore ever since the big spider was caught. Started by Sachee, even some of his own Chinatown boys start to nickname Kwang "Big Brother." Like a hero.

After a long wait with no bites Yeow swing the line hard like helicopter propeller to cast it a lot farther at an exact spot. Doing it about ten times to get there. And caught a colorful fish. It remind him of Kim who is like an angel to him ever since they meet. He saw the beautiful fish flapping for life below his feet, the hook was hard to free. He quickly used a chopstick to stir inside the dangling fish's throat to free the hook above the water. By the time it drop back into the sea Yeow is not sure if the fish will survive.

Perhaps thoughts have wings. The tropic heat cools down. On their way home from marketing in Chinatown, down No Nose Bridge, Kim blows a bubble gum in a fairy mood and ask Big Mole, "Do you like Yeow?"

"How many times you ask me that? Ha . . . !" Big Mole frown. "I am not Yeow. You ask Yeow yourself!"

Kim throws back, "Why you so angry at me like that!"

"You ask yourself," Big Mole calms down. "You talk about Yeow all the time, why . . . !" With a hand up.

"Yeow said I look nice in cowboy jeans. . . . You think so?"

"You better ask Kwang."

"Kwang is not always at home."

"But he always give you money like water."

"I am going to buy myself a pair of cowboy jeans."

"You dare to wear . . . !" Big Mole laugh at her trendy taste.

"Why not? I do what I like," Kim spit the bubble gum. "Next time I might wear high heels and put on lipsticks."

"Get the good ones," Big Mole advise. "Go to High Street."

"Chinatown also have, why go so far? Everybody give face to Yeow, he say he can get it cheaper."

"Chinatown all copy ones . . . !" Big Mole shut her up. Wondering when will Yeow really go to Penang, how to handle pushy Chai, future place with Yeow. Things she keep to herself.

By this time the tide has reach its peak and steady. Yeow make a last throw as far as possible. The moment he light another smoke, a sweeping bite caught him out of guard and flips the fishing roll out of his hand. He pounce to grab the line. It burnt his fingers, he slips and holds both hands on the roll to tackle it backward and forward for a good twenty minutes. Until a five-foot gray shark surface at the water edge.

Yeow bite tight to pull it up with all his might. Halfway up the shark escape with a splash. Daze a little, he look at his burnt finger, at the hook which has straighten. More than the jaws, it was the mean eyes of shark that tells its own tales. It remind him of Kwang.

Feeling a bit weird, he pour himself a hot coffee from the vacuum flask, eat two bean buns. And pack up for a slow long walk home.

Kwang, Sachee, and a band of spider boys just arrive at the bamboo deck when the girls was about to go out. Ah Seow is still at school, Kwang's little brothers is don't know where, eating or playing.

"Looking nice . . . !" Sachee eyes the girls. "Going where?"

"Going shopping," Kim answers with a glance at Kwang.

"Na, take some money with you." Kwang pull out his thick notes generously to flash a red ten dollar for her.

Kim snatch it and ask, "You want to come?"

Kwang scratches his head and didn't reply.

"You win again," Big Mole admire at him.

"Ya, win more today," he said with restrained pride at the attention of his spider glory. "Na, here," he push a five-dollar note into her hands. "Don't be shy with me, use some for yourself."

"No, no," Big Mole reject it.

"Take it, lah . . . !" Sachee grab it. "No need to be shy with my Big Brother, take it . . . !" insisting on her scrawny hand.

Kim also encourage. "Why you so stupid? Take it . . . !"

Big Mole took the money shyly and ask, "Sure you won't come with us?"

"Not now, lah," Kwang grin a little bit. "I have to feed and look at my spiders first."

"I am not going to wait for you then," Kim sneer at him and drag Big Mole away to buy her blue jeans at High Street which sells the latest fashion.

Although expensive she love them and wear them straightaway with a white embroidery camisole top to match.

"You dare to spend," Big Mole said outside the shop. "Where you want to go now?"

"Go home now also no use, nothing to do at home. Let's see if Yeow want to go anywhere."

When Yeow arrive at the canal boys' house the cigarette woman said at her stall, "You have just miss Big Mole and that beautiful girl."

"Which way they go? I have to catch up with Big Mole."

"You might still catch them, that way." She point across the road down the long row of one-story prewar houses.

Yeow is always cool. He took his time to wash himself up with fresh clothes. Big Mole is a familiar sight on the road leading to busier parts of Chinatown. Tracking them down with all his ears and eyes in his own territory is easy. Somebody said, "They just went inside the Seng Lee pet fish shop."

Inside the shop stacked up with many varieties of pet fishes swimming in their tanks, Yeow was shock by the shape of Kim bending down with provocative buttocks in tight blue jeans. "I like that one, and that one." She points at the bottom tanks to Big Mole biting fingernails about pet fish breeding business. It make Yeow lose his cool and pretend to watch the fishes on the other side, waiting for Kim to bum into him.

"Hey . . . !" She twist around with her old clothing in a plastic bag. "Fancy seeing you here . . . !"

"Almost can't recognize you," he smile. "You look very different, very nice in cowboy jeans . . . very nice."

Her eyes laugh. "You know how to talk!"

"Er . . . where is Kwang?"

"Kwang is living with his spiders. What for talk about him?" She reties the red handkerchief around her ponytail and ask Big Mole, "What about you? What do you want to do now?"

To protect her own rice bowl, Big Mole is very sensible. "Don't wait for me," she turn around and said. "I have to go back now, see what Sachee want to do first." To leave them alone.

Yeow use the moment and thumb at Big Mole to follow him outside the shop.

"I am going away tomorrow." He give her fifty dollars. "Can't say how long. Keep your eyes open on everybody, okay? You know what I mean?" quickly, as Kim follow out.

"I know." Big Mole took it with eyes down, with dilemma inside. Then cross the road to catch the bus home.

Piss off with Kwang, carefree Kim said straight to Yeow, "Where are you going, Bossy Face? I don't want to go home so early."

Even her voice sound sweet to his ears. He light a smoke and said, "I know the best place to eat Malay satay. Do you want to come?"

"I let you be the boss," she said with hands on the hip. "How to get there?"

"Easy." He hail a passing trishaw.

The trishaw took them to the satay center at Elizabeth Walk, a waterfront by the mouth of the Singapore River, which started the country's trading history. It was a darkly romantic place enjoy by couples.

After the satay feed the starry night was still young. They stroll and relax on a bench to watch small motorboats coughing to drag bumper boats painted with monster fish bodies and piled up with bales of rubber, into the historic river.

"Look! Look at that sampan!" Kim point to the striking different silhouette of a man standing alone to row his small boat out into the river. "I wish we can sit on one like that!"

"That is not a problem. We can hire it from Clifford Pier for a cruise around the harbor."

"Really?"

"Yes, is not far. We can walk slowly there if you like."

Kim stood up. "We might as well go now." And they stroll up the cast-iron Henderson Bridge across the Singapore River.

At Clifford Pier, below the deep-water jetty with motorboats ferrying seamen and supplies to and fro from cargo ships anchored at sea, there is a lot of old men in their sampans, moving their oars with timeless patience to stop drifting while waiting for tourist customers.

"Which one you like to pick?" Yeow ask at the jetty by the gangway down to the sea. "Pick any one you like."

"That one, that one . . . !" She point down at a cheerful old face in a big round pointed hat, waving up at her for business.

"Wave him back," Yeow stare into her excited pretty face.

She waves with her old clothing in the plastic bag. And the sampan man rows forward to hold on to the gangway for them to jump in.

Kim take the incentive to jump first, clumsy in new tight jeans with a bag in one hand. The wobbly sampan rock to one side in the choppy sea. A sudden wave cause by a motorboat make it worse, she was toss with one leg up. And fall overboard.

Yeow dive in immediately to grab her.

They crawl together up the gangway breathlessly. One side of the shoestrings on her camisole top has slip off her shoulder. A single full naked breast is vibrant just in front of Yeow's face.

By the time he sent her back later by taxi to No Nose Bridge her jeans has already shrunk up a few inches.

"Never mind!" she said boisterously, without regrets. "I can give it to Big Mole!"

And Yeow who always smile and never laugh, laugh for the first time. He laugh and laugh, like a hyena at full moon.

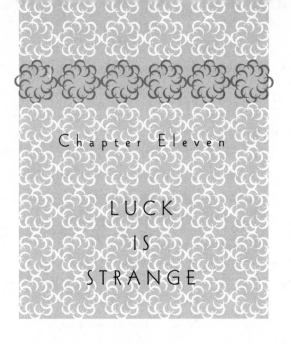

Chapter Eleven

LUCK
IS
STRANGE

Although the morning train to Penang serve good foods in the air-conditioned first-class, Yeow didn't eat much thinking of nothing but the angel-face Kim. He put on his dark glasses to watch the train passing miles and miles of rubber plantations, coconut and palm oil plantations, rice fields, and villages backgrounded by the green hills of Malaya.

When the train stopped awhile in Kuala Lumpur the movie of the Siew Jee Ho guy he killed at thirteen began to replay itself over and over in his mind. He start to wonder where his luck is heading.

Fate has a way of making things meet. It was the time of the anti-colonial period of fierce Communist uprising against the British. In the Cameron Highlands a British brigadier general had been ambushed. At Ipoh, secret police in plain clothes join the train as passengers to sniff out Communist suspects. They mingle quietly with the other travelers.

Well-dressed Yeow with dark glasses and a Rolex watch caught the attention of the British security chief who dress like a tourist in the first-class area.

"Nice watch," he comment in English inside the canteen while Yeow was having a snack. "May I share your table with you, sir?"

Yeow has no idea in English so he just smile.

The chief smile back. "Can't you speak English?"

Yeow smile again and the chief walk away.

It is always the non-English-speaking Chinese who join the Communist guerrillas under the mysterious Chin Peng. Sometimes curfews were imposed in certain areas of Ipoh, Kalantan, and Penang, which is not far from Chin Peng's headquarters along the Thai border. Well-dressed Yeow who can't speak English alerted the English chief. When the train arrives in Butterworth, at the Ferry Point of Penang, a plainclothes policeman taps him on the back and said, "Follow me."

Yeow turn around and ask, "What do you mean?"

"Police." The officer lift up his batik shirt to reveal handcuffs and a gun. And Yeow, who didn't want to be seen in handcuffs, followed him quietly into a waiting car to the Central Police Station.

After taking his photo, fingerprints, working details, identity card, and personal effects which include more than a thousand dollars in big notes, they detain him in a big crammed cell with no beds, no chairs, just straw mats to sleep.

"Hey, how long you inside here now?" he ask a decent face squatting next to him.

"Nine days today."

"Why they dump me here I don't know. . . . What about you?"

Decent Face didn't reply but ask, "Any cigarette with you?"

Yeow had a full packet. He stick one on the lips and give one across. "No matches, they took my lighter."

"I have." Decent Face dug it out like a precious object and light it carefully not to waste it.

At the same moment a rusty face from somewhere surge forward. "Whoops!" He blew out the light and demand with a finger, "What about me? Pass one over . . . !"

"Nah . . . !" Yeow snarl. "Take the whole fucking packet!" Throwing it high in the air for him to catch.

A quick hand from somewhere snatch it from the air.

"Is mine!" And a fight break out between two dogs. One is Siew Jee Ho gang, the other Kun Thong gang member.

Decent Face is a half-crazy man who can't stand fighting. He bangs at the cell door. "Hey! Hey! Hey!" continuously until the guards rush in to collar the two dogs away.

Food is like pig feed. Lights is switch off early. To prevent bedbugs under the mats crawling all over the body, Yeow squat-sleep with elbows on the knees. All the detainees were picked up at random with no reasons given under Section 55 of the new law, which allow detention without trial. Every day busloads of people fill up the cells. Special agents is planted in every cell to seek out suspects.

The next morning when the underground cell doors bang open many are transferred. Newcomers like Yeow are given the task of cleaning toilets. Some are sent for identification parades, some for questioning. Many are freed and new ones take their place.

One newcomer from the old street days glance around and spotted Yeow.

"Hey...! Are you Smiling Boy?" he ask surprised. "You disappear, long time no see. Where you been?" he demand with a frown.

"What do you mean?" Yeow purposely scowl back at him. "You must be looking at the wrong person." And move away cursing inside for being discovered.

The next day is the same. Some were freed, new lots came in. On the third day another newcomer from the old street days turn up. "Hey," he said to his mate. "That smooth-looking guy is Smiling Boy. Have you talk to him?"

"Aarrh, fuck him...! I ask, he said he is not."

"Two eyes can't be wrong, wonder why he lie? I ask him."

"What for? He don't want to know us."

At the opposite end of the one-bus-long space, half bus length wide, Yeow pretend he hear and see nothing. He kill time by observing everybody quietly at a distance. This caught the attention of a spy who smokes beside him and ask, "Hey, you have any visitor?" Looking well fed and no worries on the face.

Yeow was ready for him.

"No," he answer tamely. "I am from Singapore. . . . I don't know why I am here."

"Smoke?" the spy offer him one and start to ask questions.

Yeow feed the undercover in their midst, about picking up his auntie's bones, how he was arrested for no reason, about his legal business as a newspaper distributor. The calculated talks paid off when the spy made his report. Yeow was free the next day after a brief questioning.

It was the English chief from the train who sign the release paper. "Strikes me as an interesting chap," he said to his Chinese assistant. "Have you checked with the CID in Singapore?"

"Yes, sir," the Chinese assistant answer. "He is clean, sir, no record."

"I still can't make out the Chinese," the chief admit. "Tell me, what do you make of him?"

"I think he live on girls, sir. A pimp."

"I suppose you are right." The chief smoke his pipe with a Sherlock Holmes face under a high ceiling fan in his office on the top floor with window looking down several streets at once.

Down below, Yeow felt his detention was just bad luck, a case of mistaken identity. On the other hand he was also glad to outfox the spy. The new confidence make him feel he can outsmart anybody. Because the Special Branch is well paid and is uncorrupted he even get back all his belongings, including the money and his pocketknife attached to his key ring.

Outside the Central Police Station busy with lots of people queuing to inquire about their friends and relatives, the old trishaw men wait for customers. They jostle their trishaws forward for business.

"Hey . . . ! Hey . . . ! Where you going . . . ? Where you going . . . ?"

Yeow hop in one. "Queen Hotel," he said from memory of the expensive hotel with no gangs hanging around.

"How much?" he ask on arrival.

"Three dollars." The trishaw man wipe the sweats with a towel over the shoulder.

Although he know the price is cutthroat, Yeow pay and said, "What about pick me up here tomorrow morning, around nine?"

"To where?"

"Cantonese cemetery, wait around an hour and return?"

"Seven dollars all together, alright?"

Yeow feel generous and didn't bargain at the crazy tourist price. The path on the way is too narrow for a taxi. He was looking forward to saying grace at his auntie's grave before making the necessary arrangement for the bones to be dig out. In his early Penang days when the going gets too tough he always went quietly to her grave to grieve and complain. This make him feel better again.

Although dirty, hungry, and tired from sleepless nights, the first thing he did was make a toll call to Singapore.

"I am glad you call," Cigarette Woman answer. "How are you?"

"Everything is quite smooth," Yeow say to avoid her worrying. "What about things over there?"

"Fine, where are you staying?"

"The Queen Hotel."

"Just in case, what is your hotel number?"

Yeow read her the number and said, "Don't worry about me."

"Bring some Ipoh peanuts back ...!" she demand before putting down the phone.

* * *

After a good bath and a meal Yeow sleep soundly. Early the next morning a loud bomb blast shake the hotel. A waitress in the kitchen spills her tray. "The mountain rats have done it again . . . !"

A bomb planted by the Communists has exploded near the famous clock tower, not far from the Queen Hotel. Fire engines and police cars were screaming everywhere. Inside the hotel lobby Yeow overheard a staff member caution a friendly guest, "Don't go out too soon. The police is setting up roadblocks everywhere to catch people anyhow like crazy!"

When his trishaw arrive, Yeow paid him for nothing and book for the following morning. The trishaw man pedaled away happily on his lucky day to gamble four color cards at Trishaw Lane.

Inside the Central Police Station people continue to be freed or brought in for detention. Yeow's name already slip out and chain reacts. He becomes something to talk about among all the ex-street boys who have grown up into different gangs.

The story of the gold shop job and the guy killed in Kuala Lumpur resurface. They add one and one together like detectives. It reach the ears of the Siew Jee Ho gang with a leader who never forget how their mate died. "Revenge for each other mates us together," is his philosophy at nearly forty.

"I don't know much about that smooth-looking guy," he admit as he eat with some of his men. "But what the fuck make him bluff he is not Smiling Boy?"

"Must be him," a member insist. "Can't be wrong . . . !"

Another ask, "Where is the smooth-looking guy now?"

"See those trishaw guys at Central," suggest a big guy with a mouthful of rice and meat. "They will know."

"Find him first, then we talk," the chief gesture with his chopstick. And pick out the biggest chili prawn for himself.

The trishaw patch at the Central Police Station was part of their give-face territory to those trishaw men who were friendly with them. After a few inquiries it didn't take long for Big Guy to find the driver. Both were gambling addicts and knew each other quite well.

After Big Guy make his report, the Siew Jee Ho chief said, "He must be doing well to live in that expensive hotel. . . . I guess it is Smiling Boy, must be him."

Nobody disagree.

Big Guy added, "That trishaw driver is on our side, he say there are two ways to Cantonese Cemetery Hill."

The chief said, "Let him pick his own way," and all the members felt bound together in a mission like religion.

The next morning trishaw man arrive exactly on time. The clock tower not far away strikes, "*Tong . . . ! Tong . . . ! Tong . . . !*" clearly nine times, the moment Yeow took his seat. Trishaw man lift up the adjustable canvas over customer's head to shade against the sun.

"Is hot today," he pretend to give good service. "There are two ways to Cantonese Cemetery Hill. Which way you like?"

With a red shirt on for good luck, Yeow put on his dark glasses. "That way," he point toward the clock tower in bustling Georgetown.

Passing gang corners, memory lanes, all the way out of a busy market street full of trishaws waiting for customers. The trishaw man pedaled slowly and wipes his sweat with an orange towel. And Big Guy with two others follow them on bicycles.

Bicycles make no noise. In a quiet track between trees they speed up to stop the trishaw. The trishaw man put up a false struggle, Yeow dash out of his seat. Big Guy from behind swing him down to kiss the ground. The next moment he was tied up and stuffed inside a big jute sack used for bagging charcoal. Dumped back like cargo in the trishaw. While the trishaw man calmly rides Big Guy's bicycle in the opposite direction.

Big Guy pedaled the trishaw to an old two-story wooden house inside a dying coconut plantation waiting for redevelopment. Motorbikes and bicycles were parked outside. Two dogs chained under a rambutan tree bark at their arrival.

A member come out and yell, "Got the pig!"

Big Guy lift up his left foot from the pedal and kick the sack. "Is here!" he answers proudly and brakes so the sack is thrown forward.

Inside the house was the old canteen with long benches and tables used in the past by workers, with sleeping space upstairs. About a dozen gang members were waiting for the occasion. They all crowd round when the chief unties the sack.

"Let's see if he is Smiling Boy or not," he said and pulled out the rag stuffed in Yeow's mouth.

Yeow felt his soul has aborted. He knew they want blood. He recognize a few street boys who has joined them, some close friends of the guy killed in Kuala Lumpur. When his rope was cut loose they tease him. "Are you Smiling Boy? Recognize me? Recognize your uncle? Can you smile . . . ?"

"No . . . ! I am not!" he deny vigorously to create a cloud of doubt. "You all looking at the wrong person."

"So many eyes can't be wrong...!" A hot-tempered guy jump up and shakes his teacup ears. "Are you real? Are you real?"

"People can look the same," Yeow cast more doubts. "Who is Smiling Boy? Make sure you get the right people...!" And stood up to strip off the Rolex, take out all his more than one thousand dollars in hundred-dollar notes.

"Is that what you all want?" He put it on the long table, including the thick gold chain around his neck.

Money change the situation.

"You have just earn yourself a place to sit. Sit down," said the deputy with the lame leg who then gesture to the chief for a private talk outside the house.

"Something worth thinking," Lame Leg said. "The water [money] on the table is not small. That smooth guy is easy with it."

"I know what you mean," the chief reply. "But we don't sell the rules. All our brothers has to get the facts straight."

"Sure, but nothing has change. Better to bleed the water before we bleed his blood."

The chief think and said, "Alright. How?"

"Lock him up first, give him time to think.... Let him find his own answers. I am sure he will buy himself out. That smooth pig has a lot of oil!"

It make sense. And Yeow was lock inside the empty storeroom built under the stairway leading up to the first floor.

Then Lame Leg divides up the cash. Everybody was happy. It was money they didn't expect.

"We have a proper talk tonight." The chief keep the thick gold chain. "More of our brothers are coming."

Inside the long narrow cell under the stairway Yeow can hear their motorbikes pumping them away. He was glad to get away without being searched, they were all looking at the money. The three-inch knife and the lighter are still inside his pocket. To find out how many is on guard, he bangs the door hard. "Hey! Hey! Hey!" he shout, like the half-mad man inside the police station.

The three guards cutting up pineapple to eat with tattooed hands jump up and rush over. One of them open the door.

Yeow shout for reaction.

"What am I here for!"

"Don't fuck around with me...." The second guard push him inside with a two-feet water pipe.

"One more noise, I slice your mouth with this," the third guard warn with a razor-sharp pineapple knife ten inches long. And slam the door nailed with a sliding lock.

Inside the storeroom, under its sloping ceiling, besides the spider-webs were piles of old newspaper. Yeow stack it up and stand on it with his lighter to survey the old plywood roof boxed under the plank floor above. He dig the rotten part with his pocket knife until light filter through the gaps in the planks above. After about an hour of quiet careful work he stuff crumpled-up newspaper inside then rest awhile to calm himself down. And light the fire.

The flames roar upward to catch oxygen as he calculated, he lay under the door at the low opposite end to breathe. As the smokes get thicker and hot to breathe, he heard the running shouts of "Fire! Fire!" by the guards rushing up to the top floor to check.

Yeow gripped his pocketknife and kicked at the point of the door lock. It burst apart. Dashing out of the house, he saw a bicycle parked against a fence and ran toward it. The two dogs barked madly under the rambutan tree and the guard with the pineapple knife rushed at him.

Instinct takes over. Pineapple thrust his ten-inch blade forward into Yeow's belly. Yeow swing up his small knife into Pineapple's armpit and pull! Pineapple stagger backward, dropping his knife. Simultaneously, Yeow double up to avoid the pineapple knife which still pierce through his side belly a few inches away from his belly button.

In the split moment, Yeow saw the other two guards panicking out of the old long house burning like dry leaves. He force himself up with the strength of desperation on the bicycle. And bike for his life as fast as he can. Once he hit the main road and saw people again he felt giddy and then finally faint from loss of blood.

In the hospital Yeow told the police he was robbed by unknown attackers. He phone Singapore and Cigarette Woman's husband, Cheong Pak, flew over immediately and fly him back after a week spent in hospital bed. When the plane landed in Singapore, Yeow's face was still pale from the narrow escape. Cheong Pak said with his hands full with all the luggage, "Your health come first, I have arranged a quiet place by Katong Beach for you to have a proper rest."

"Just bad luck," Yeow shake his head in disgust. "I don't want anybody to know what has happen to me in Penang, okay?"

In the rich area of Katong even the police look polite. The new place, a tidy bungalow fenced by thick shrubs, is very private. Yeow love it at first sight and start quietly to recuperate, thinking of lost face with his auntie's bones, and also of Kim.

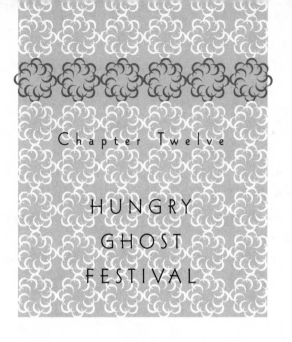

Chapter Twelve

HUNGRY GHOST FESTIVAL

Midterm school holiday begin. The Hungry Ghost Festival is coming soon. Chinese temples in every part of Singapore were busy organizing their annual opera shows of ancient stories to appease the lost souls set free by the King of Hell for a month holiday. "Ancestor worship is a must," state the blind man of the Kuan Yin Temple. "Better for them, better for us."

Desperate people worships their religion harder. The village were full of desperadoes. The day before the Ghost Festival starts on the first full moon of the seventh lunar month, pigs scream under the knives in the small communities within the community, who make joint efforts to buy a pig, chickens, cook foods, make cakes, patiently folding up joss stick papers into the image of a small boat with a cone in the middle, working out the amount of coins to be thrown away as part of the sacrifice to please and stop angry hungry ghosts from haunting them.

When popular Wong who manages the annual show pass the hat around, everybody give face. Donations from all sorts pour in for the Kuan Yin Temple to stage a three-day, three-night opera show on the playground. Blind Man and his wife welcome hired nuns and tankies (mediums) into the temple to perform rituals.

On the first festival morning the whole village was vibrating. Giant incenses that take three men to carry has arrived. The opera stage was setting up. Opera actors, actresses, musicians, and makeup artists arrive with gypsy hawkers from elsewhere to boost the occasion.

The annual champion-of-champions spider matching competition is held soon after the Hungry Ghost Festival. Hard-core spider boys in other districts of Singapore roam about to check the best places for coin scrambling, to bet on the approaching Spider Olympic Games. Spider fever were brewing up everywhere. Legendary tales of how spiders fought in the past were talk about again and again under the huge banyan tree. Somebody say, "Have you heard of a small La Sap Pow [Dirty Trick] who don't war dance, but just pounce and bite off the arms of other big ones to become king?"

"Like you . . . !" a small watermelon boy point at Sachee.

Other eyes turn around at Ah Seow who try to hang around.

Ah Seow felt his arm scarred by Sachee's bites and walk away bitterly from the disgrace. Life was a drag for Ah Seow to walk alone. San, his best friend, was busy helping his father Wong to manage the show.

In the late afternoon. Inside the Kuan Yin Temple amidst smoky incense and glowing oil lamps, sounds of bells, cymbals, gongs, and chanting of nuns starts to make the exotic dressed mediums turn their heads round and round faster and faster into a trance before the main altar of life-size Kuan Yin, Goddess of Mercy, and her half-dozen, half-life-size demigods, caste in bronze.

The sounds of gongs and drums gets louder and louder. Thick crowds waited outside when the moon just come out. Spider boys jostle about for the best position for the coin throwing. Ah Seow was there but Chai was in town.

Kwang, who love the fun, push his way with Sachee to the front.

"Get ready!" Kwang shout. "Tankies coming out soon . . . ! See how much you can make!"

"I won't lose face," Sachee boast in a pouncing posture with a cheap look at Ah Seow.

A burst of gongs and cymbals and drums by nuns leads out the procession of eight seminaked tankies in a trance with painted faces, jerking backward and forward with daggers through their tongues, spears through their cheeks, follow by pallbearers carrying small shrines seated with idols of demigods, representing the trancing mediums. Waiting worshipers follow behind the procession and dip their hands into the coin buckets to sprinkle left and right anywhere they like.

Boys pounce and scramble for it like mad. Nuggety Sachee fought hard. Every time he pounce, he tumbles by the pushing and rushing forces of bigger boys and get nowhere.

When the ceremony in front of the temple is over, the mediums and helpers cross the road toward the opera stage at the playground, to bless the place.

"Make any eats . . . ?" Kwang grin at Sachee. "You tumble like a watermelon . . . !"

"Few cents only . . . !" Sachee shakes it in his hand.

"You feel here. Here . . . !" Kwang taps at his pocket full of coins and scoop out a handful of copper and silver.

"Waah!" Sachee exclaim. "Five cents and ten cents too . . . !"

Kwang lift up his shorts to rubber band around the pockets of coins to prevent them falling out in the next scramble. And teach, "Next time watch the eyes of the coin thrower, not their hands . . . ! They throw where their eyes see. Stamp your feet on the silver first, don't pounce down with your hands, you get push over! That is why you tumble like a watermelon, get nothing!" And make Sachee laugh at his own image a while ago.

Some boys were still searching for the missed-out coins. Among them is Ah Seow who pretend to search to hear what they say.

"Is getting dark," Sachee said to Kwang. "Where to go now?"

Ah Seow whiz a thought. He decided to swallow his pride and join in. "Chai's grandmother is throwing a lot of coins at their gambling house, more than Fatty's Family's place." Purposely.

"I know," Kwang nod. "Don't waste time, follow me."

"No!" Sachee reply. "No, I don't want to go to Chai's house, I want to go and find Big Mole at your house."

"Up to you, see you later," Kwang said and jog away to catch up for the next round.

Coin scramblings were for bigger boys. Sachee with no small friends around wonders what to do by himself in the new environment of the village as night fall. Blaze a look at Ah Seow.

"Only my father is at home," Ah Seow play friendly and lies. "My sister and Big Mole went out with Shark Head's little brothers. Where you want to go?"

"You know where they go?" Sachee ask reluctantly with a guilty look for biting Ah Seow's arm.

"Can be anywhere in one of my sister's friend's places. Want to go together? Come on . . . !" Ah Seow wave brotherly.

Grown up in the cities, Sachee, a town boy, is use to have people around him and was still quite green in Ho Swee Hill. He follow Ah Seow halfheartedly.

Ah Seow felt for his six-inch coffin nail against Pontianak spirits at night. He lead Sachee from the heart of the village to the farming areas at mid-hill.

Sachee stop and ask, "Where are you going?"

"Going uphill," Ah Seow smile. "I show you a new place for pet fish breeding first. . . . Look for Big Mole and everyone later. They all sure to go to the Pau Kung show at eight. Want to come?"

"How far to go?"

"Halfway there already."

"I want to find Big Mole first."

"Who is Big Mole?" Ah Seow poke as they walk uphill. "She is not your sister, not your mother, too big to be your girlfriend. Why you always follow her?"

The cunning insult open up a weak spot Sachee cannot grasp and never aware before. His vibrant and bold personality weaken with a new pain. He shy away from Ah Seow's eyes towering down at him and walk faster ahead stompily on a narrow path in between atap houses under the bright moonlight.

Ah Seow was thrill to see him suffer. His intention was to lead him astray. "Sachee . . . !" he shout from behind. "Turn left! Turn left!"

The left turn leads to a few more twist and turns uphill into an isolated track going to a dead end with a rotten, broken-down wooden gate almost invisible by the long lalang grass among tall cempaka trees looming spaciously apart. Wary Sachee stops and turn around to face the approaching Ah Seow.

"Do you know where you are?" Ah Seow ask cautiously. "There is a pond and a house with nobody inside, good place to breed fighting fish."

Sachee's survival on the streets sense is powerful. He felt Ah Seow was up to something. He steal a glance at Ah Seow's sensitive parts and sideways at their shadows cast by the full moon.

Ah Seow spoke, "You scare? If scare we go back now . . . !"

Sachee's pride never die. "What to scare! Inside here?" He squeeze through the half-open rotten gate.

"Ya . . . ! The pond is inside there." Ah Seow point forward.

Sachee brushes aside the long lalang grasses that is taller than him on the old track. "Can't see . . . !" he said. "You taller than me, you go inside first."

Reluctantly, Ah Seow led the way to the edge of the small pond which is too wet for long lalang grasses, and all clear across the pond beautiful by the reflection of the moon pearl upon it. Beauty dissolves vengeance. Ah Seow felt uncertain. He start to look at Sachee with a new light and point at a run-down hut under a jumboo tree. "Shark Head caught a big spider there long ago."

"Check it out later." Sachee switches his rabbit eyes back on the pond waving silvery currents by light breeze, disturbing the tranquillity, beautiful to both of them dreaming about breeding pet fishes. And draw them to oneness by the scene before them, which has floating water lilies carpeting half of the pond around.

A second gust of winds brought some cempaka flowers down from the tall trees. When this very sweet-smelling flower falls, it release its best smells.

Sachee sniffs. "Smells nice," he said. "Maybe Big Mole like it?" Delightly and scramble toward a cempaka fallen on top of a patch of floating water lily on the pond. He pushes away the water lily, deeper to reach his flower.

Ah Seow's psyche felt something wrong. Ghost looking for replacement touches him on Halloween night. Spooky feeling squeezes out unknown sensitivities. "Sachee!" he scream out. "There is a water ghost in the pond! Don't go in! Don't go in!"

Sachee felt Ah Seow is making false alarm to frighten him for a gutsful joke. He play brave to grab his cempaka flower, got it, and turn around with a froggy face sticking out his tongue, waving his flower.

"Ooohoo . . . ! Ooohoo . . . ! Ooohoo . . . !" Howling step by step toward Ah Seow for kicks.

What is not real for Sachee is very real for Ah Seow's psyche. Ah Seow felt Sachee has turn into a water ghost, everything become darker with more shadows. The serene moonlight pond is no more beautiful, but awful and alive.

Time stand still. The rustling breeze is not cool but cold, heart pumping faster, the long lalang grasses rustle more in shadows, the ripe jumboo fruits falling to the ground by occasional stronger winds was then sharper to his ears. Ah Seow didn't miss any sounds, sounds that related to fear beats the loudest. His legs melt down to watery weak and can't stand up, thoughts of "as safe as a house" race in his mind. "Run! Run! Run!" he mantra to hypnotize himself, begin to crawl madly toward the run-down hut, blindly.

Sachee catch up and grab one of his leg. "Stop playing a fool! Look! Look at the jumboo tree in front of the house!"

Ah Seow think Sachee is the water ghost. "Not me . . . ! Not me . . . !" he cry for mercy and buried his face down.

Sachee pull him up by the back collar. "Look!" he point ahead. "Look! Somebody hanging on the jumboo tree!"

Ah Seow feel better when their faces meet and bring him back to reality. He looks. . . . One look is enough to tell him that Chai's grandmother, Ah Paw, was the corpse hanging on the jumboo tree with eyes and tongue choking out on her black samfoo suit.

The past, of her trying to rape him, wheels into his being. He black out into a blinding darkness illuminated by multiplying stardusts, stardusts disappear into total darkness, darkness evaporates into nothingness, nothingness becomes vacuum and voids into an inexhaustible whirlpool, sucking his consciousness into bottomless space. Like the essence of his inner spirit were draining away forever and ever into eternity, haunted by the eternal torture of no control, yearning to stop, yearning to be touch by something, anything! Vegetables, minerals, something to give sensation back, even a dust particle is desirable. . . . Into the realm of untouchable desires yearning to be touchable. Into a mystery trip of ghost world control by fiends.

There, all the ghosts have nothing to do and cannot do anything. All they do is watch TV. Earth looks to them like the jewel of the universe. Every time they see friends and relatives on Earth, they get a buzz. Every buzz makes them sadder. And it makes the fiends laugh.

Ah Seow in the world of strange happenings then drifts his astral consciousness like a flash back to Earth. And fainted in front of Sachee, who race downhill to the house with a bamboo deck.

Everybody was out, even Ah Seow's solitary father, Ah Hock. Sachee gasp for breath and race again. He race to the opera show. He can't find them. The showground was packed with people watching the opera of Lord Pau Kung, the legendary clairvoyant judge, who was preparing to execute the prime minister's son who murder his wife to marry the emperor's sister.

Ah Seow's astral consciousness was attracted to the show. He was watching the action on stage. He has no idea about his own real body lying before the corpse of Ah Paw dangling on the jumboo tree.

When the opera was over the thick crowd disperse for the great variety of food hawked by gypsy hawkers who follow the troupe, but Ah Seow took the opportunity to watch the actresses in the changing room behind the stage.

Sachee finally found Big Mole and Kim with Kwang and his little brothers walking home with a bunch of spider boys.

"Looking for you all everywhere!" Sachee throws up his frustrations. "We must go and save Ah Seow!" And tell his story quickly.

"You all go home first." Kwang wave away the girls and his little brothers and said to his spider boys, "Dare to come with me?"

They follow their leader up the hill. One look at Ah Paw was enough to make everybody vomit, no matter how brave. Nobody dare to touch Chai's grandmother's body.

"Look at Ah Seow first!" Sachee the guilty one said. "Ah Seow is dead . . . ! Ah Seow . . . ! Ah Seow!" Shaking Ah Seow whose body is still warm. But who don't wake up.

"Don't say such things!" Kwang anger at Sachee. "We lift him up, don't be scared! Give us a hand!" Yelling at his boys who number more than a dozen.

They rush over to carry Ah Seow to the pond side. Kwang listen to his heartbeats and said hastily, "Still breathing! Quick, get some pond water first!"

Water was splashed on Ah Seow's face with Po Kure leaves. Still they can't revive him.

"Ah Seow dead already!" Sachee sniffs. His sobs make Kwang and the others cry also around Ah Seow's body.

It was past midnight. The village sleeps. There was nothing much for the ghost of Ah Seow to look at. He was on his way home to sleep with Big Mole and his sister yawning by a kerosene lamp on the bamboo deck. He could hear his father snoring after an extra bottle of Guinness. Everything seemed normal.

Then the sobbing grief of Kwang and his boys disturbs his senses.

His astral consciousness follows the sounds at the speed of light to the spot. He wonders why they are there. Why is everybody weeping over a body?

"Carry him up!" Kwang order. "Take him home first!"

Ah Seow take a close look, he saw himself. He panic and jump into his own body. But he can't, he slips out of it.

Sachee the guilty one continues to cry. Grief turns to anger and braver than the rest. "Not Ah Seow," he said. "That old woman is a devil . . . ! So many of us here . . . ! Why scare!" He stumbles through the lalangs and yanks at Ah Paw's dangling leg. The pull release a gas with a terrible smell, a smell locked up in a body choked to death, like all hanged corpses do.

Like by a magic spell, the stench projects watching Ah Seow back into his own body which becomes freezing cold. It burns like dry ice sizzling, mist steams up around it. The mist turn into water and he saw two big carp fishes swimming with their mouths open, singing, "Human flesh is divine, divine . . . !" then Ah Seow kick and scream himself back to life.

He stand up and walk with a loony face like wanky drunk. Everybody try to talk to him at once. There was no reply. Sachee hold his hand, he didn't resist.

Hand in hand they walk together downhill. The rest follows behind on the first Halloween night.

Before the morning was over, the death of Ah Paw hush the whole village. She was a living legend, the oldest person known. A busybody whisper to another, "Do you believe it . . . ? On the same night her pair of big carp fish jump out of the tank to suicide!"

And then, "This is real! A lot of regulars in their gambling house saw it. . . . You can ask Gentleman Pak's wife, she was there. She wouldn't tell lies!"

Some said, "She poison the fish to die with her." But others said, "It can't be. How come the three goldfishes belong to old Big Head is still alive in the same tank?"

Although the mystery remain, Ah Seow return back to normal. He become good friends with Sachee who accompany him all that night.

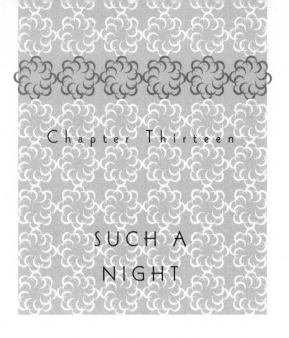

Chapter Thirteen

SUCH A NIGHT

The weather has change. The monsoon season brings rain. It is a low period for spider catching or matching, the time to train spiders for the Spider Olympic Games. Like other top spider boys throughout Singapore, Kwang stay at home on rainy days to train his spiders, making them fight for food, fight for female spiders. Watching all their actions with his magnifying glass on the bamboo deck. His little brothers were swimming in the rain in flooding muddy pools with Sachee doing the teaching while Ah Seow was at school.

On the table of the deck was a pot of sweet potato soup boiled in rock sugar. Big Mole, who begin to run out of money, said to Kim, "I feel very disturb inside, do you think anything bad has happened to Yeow?" And scoops the soup into the bowls.

"Waiting is hard," Kim reply and taste the soup, thinking of Yeow privately. It is something she can't control from the day she fall overboard at Clifford Pier, something that make her less carefree, change from extrovert to introvert as life develop around her.

Big Mole stares at the soup and said, "No mood to eat." Sick inside from relying on Yeow's peanut money for spying everything for him about Kwang and Kim, including where Wong get and smoke opium, which she still don't know. Being Yeow's eyes make her feel worry and dirty inside. She look at Kwang, who will be fifteen in a few more months, scruffy like her.

Kwang close up the box with the big spider inside and join the table. "You eat first," he assure Big Mole. "Don't worry, Yeow is very alert." Looking forward to spider games, becoming champion of champions in the coming Olympics, confident of himself like hell. And Kim getting more and more pissed off with his obsession.

On the other side of the equation, life for Yeow was also changing. After his narrow escape from death, the lone wolf has lived quietly alone for more than two months. He feel like he is on top of the globe. Even his secret desire for Kim, even his auntie's bones, don't bother him anymore. Every day he go fishing and swimming at the beach. His health is good, his mind is clear, his heart is firm. Firmly on a waiting game for Kwang to win the spider crown first.

Yeow is an incredibly patient young man who think like an old man, who has a vision. For he saw the fish must grow by itself before he net it. The picture is very clear to the empire dreamer plotting his dominion beyond Chinatown via the hard-core spider boys in every corner of Singapore, stepping-stones to reach his goal.

Spider boys already roam like gangs in control of their own territories. They all listen to the one who wears the crown.

"Good thinking," said Cheong Pak, with a newspaper rolled up in front of Yeow. "He is their hero. You got him, you get the rest. . . . How many of them are there altogether? Roughly?"

"Thousands of them, scatter everywhere." Yeow relax on the posh leather couch. "Only the best are at the match, Chai said hundreds there last year."

"What is Kwang's chance? I mean . . . winning the crown?"

"Very good, according to Chai."

"Good horse is not easy to catch, be flexible with him . . . !"

"I know, I will bend backward if he win to trap him."

"Right," Cheong Pak nod. "Bend like bamboo against the wind." And walk away to make coffee in the big expensive kitchen.

Beside Chai, who only lately learn of his whereabout, Cheong Pak and his wife is Yeow's only visitors. They serve their protégé like a willing slave, teaching him everything they know. From the art of war by the ancient military genius Sun–Tzu, who say, "Know yourself, know your enemy . . . a thousand battle fought, a thousand battle won." To the strategy of building a business empire for a new Hon Moon.

Hon Moon (Red Gate) was created by the Kuomintang in China with a mission to raise funds from overseas Chinese for Sun Yatsen to topple the Manchu dynasty. Wong's father very important in its organization there. Their biggest money earner in Singapore is Chap Jee Kee (Twelve Sticks), an illegal lottery for people to bet at night and wait for result next day. Poor people hooked on it like drugs, live life just to play. Although Hon Moon extinguish itself and Wong retire when China turn red under Mao, Chap Jee Kee resurface under control of faceless people. Almost every Chinese family in Singapore have someone who play.

Wizard-face Cheong Pak is a shortish stalky man who walk straight like a soldier at nearly sixty. He comes back with the coffee ready and said, "Don't get me wrong. I know you are trying to put your feet into the network of Chap Jee Kee through those spider boys, but you have to admit we are far from ready yet. Chap Jee Kee are bigger than the bank! Climb the hill before you climb the mountain.... We should make other investments first."

"Such as?" said Yeow, ambitious but willing to listen.

"Like buy this place."

"How much you talking?" Yeow pour the coffee in the cups.

"Close to fifty thousand dollars."

"I can't see how we make ... the rent here is only one hundred fifty."

"Cash must go into assets." Cheong Pak sip his coffee. "We are overflowed with unaccounted cash on our hands. The owner is willing to take half in cash, the rest through proper channels.... Property price here is rising fast. Is up to you."

"Go ahead, buy," Yeow yawn and raise the coffeepot, thinking further. "More coffee?"

After Cheong Pak left, Yeow went for a swim. When dry, he make a phone call.

"Hello?" A Eurasian-Chinese girl answer in English. "Ng Koo's villa. Can I help?"

"I don't speak English." Yeow twiddle his toes on the stolen antique table inlay with mother-of-pearl. "Do me a favor, get Ng Koo for me, okay?"

"Ng Koo is busy at the moment. . . . May I know who is calling?"

"Just tell her is from Chinatown Yeow, okay?" And put down the phone to check his fishing gear.

Ng Koo is the widow of a rich Englishman. She organize social functions round a top-class secret brothel in Pasir Panjang and use young housewives, office girls, secretaries who spend beyond their means. When Yeow called she was entertaining some British and Chinese millionaires. The moment the Eurasian girl whisper to her boss, Ng Koo excuse herself and phone him immediately.

Yeow push his hooks and lines aside.

"Hello, Number Twenty-one." Using the street address and not his name.

"Yeow," Ng Koo heave up her body on the sofa. "I have been trying to catch up with you."

Yeow twiddle his toes again. "So what is new?"

"A few nice girls have just arrive."

"So?"

"I prefer you to be the first to know."

"What else?"

"Hey, you don't sound your usual self . . . ! How are you?"

"Not shining very bright." Yeow think of something to say. "A bit stretched out from swimming. . . ."

"You need a massage," Ng Koo answer quickly. Come over. . . . I polish you up myself!"

"I can smell your perfume from here."

"And I can read your mind from where I am. Come over tonight, alright?"

Ng Koo was introduced to Yeow weeks earlier by a chauffeur friend who worked for rich businessmen who frequent her place. Yeow has been planning to get closer to her to use her in whatever way possible, but as yet don't know how. That evening he go to her house in the superrich area of Pasir Panjang on the cliff above a long beach. It is a prewar Spanish mansion with high walls and wrought-iron gates through which he can see the compound parked full of flash cars. The lone wolf is dress up in his best, press the bell three times, the hunchback gatekeeper come out and let him in. He tip the old fellow a dollar and is led into a candlelit hall with tables spread with fine foods, drinks, and soft music playing. It is a party atmosphere with more young girls than men, both European and Chinese enjoying themselves while talking business.

The moment Ng Koo saw Yeow sitting quietly on the sofa by the French doors she pass her drink to one of her girls and say, "Aah, Lily . . . the prince has arrive! Come with me." On high heels and in brocade cheongsam she lead her to him.

"You don't have to be shy with him," Ng Koo touch Yeow's handsome chin with her long red fingernails. "Mr. Yeow is much more shy than you, make him a drink!" And whisper in his ear, "I catch up with you later." She move away with her hands squeezing the pearl necklace against her full breast rubbed with pure musk perfume from Tibet.

Yeow was fascinated by the charming widow who has travel the world, especially the way she know her way around top circles. But the spunky part-time secretary is saying, "Mr. Yeow, can I get you a drink?"

He turn around. "What?" Drunk already from Ng Koo's classy spell.

"Can I get you something to drink?" Lily ask again.

Yeow request a whiskey sour and keep watching Ng Koo pouring drinks for her clients, making sure everyone is happy. Sometimes she will say, "Don't get drunk, George (or Jimmy, or Lee, or Mr. Chan)!" Or, "Hmmm, naughty, naughty!" with a finger playfully on the nose of an old client who try to touch her body, trim from playing endless tennis. Shrewd like a vixen, she charge a lot per client just for the party. But not for the girls who are her baits, only room fees if they use her five bedrooms.

Lily sees his interest and try to start a conversation.

"Don't you think Ng Koo is amazing? I really admire her."

"I am not sure what you mean," Yeow look at his Rolex.

"Are you staying long tonight?" Lily sip her orange juice.

"I am not sure, depends." He knock back the whiskey sour.

"You are very quiet."

"Am I?"

"Yes, and distant."

"Distant? No," Yeow go straight to the point. "I am not use to this place. Everybody is talking in English I can't understand. Only my third time here. . . . I rather have fun with you."

She get a key from Ng Koo and take him to a sea-view room upstairs, with specially built beanbag chairs for sex. Although she is beautiful, sex which money can buy is to Yeow just like another piece of cold meat to eat when hungry. When it was over, he ask the price. It was fifty dollars. He give her sixty and said, "I feel like lying down here for a while by myself, alright? Let Ng Koo know if it is okay." To send an indirect message to the widow.

Downstairs Ng Koo introduce Lily to an old millionaire who later whisk her away in a Mercedes. Yeow was smoking on the bed when she walk in, changed to a transparent silk gown. She pinch the cigarette away with a smacky kiss on his lips.

"I am relieved the party is over." She kill the smoke on the bedside ashtray. "I am sick of making money." And lean over to massage his toes.

"I promise to give you a massage, didn't I?" Her face is skillfully brushed with makeup, like a piece of art that erase her age, mysterious and inviting like the musk perfume on her tempting breast, heaving, as she work her way up with her hands and mouth over his baby skin.

It makes his whole body shivers. And he licks and sucks her breasts hungrily like never enough. Then she place herself on top of him, and pumps with the sound of rushing wave below doing the music. Until herself drop flat with ecstasy.

Then he turn her over slowly and ride her like a beast with clench teeth harder and harder, her long red fingernails anchor on his back. She tighten and tighten until he explode with overflows into her wriggling body electrified by the young wolf.

Even when it was all over, her legs was still spreading out like asking for more, his overflows dripping out of her vagina. And the sailing clouds through the big window cover up the moon, making the night pitch-dark.

On the opposite side of such a night in the soggy bottom of Ho Swee Hill is a small room with old newspapers covering up the gaps in rough plank walls between close-knitted neighbors. Big Mole was thinking hard about the coming-soon rent on her collapsible canvas bed, a few feet away from Sachee on his. In between them on the hard mud floor was a burning mosquito coil keeping the mosquitoes away. The mosquitoes is terrible, especially when it rains in the day and there is no winds at night. They swarm out from everywhere. Sachee smacks at them against his chubby face and hides under the thin blanket.

"Big Mole, Big Mole," he cry. "One coil is not enough . . . ! Burn another one!"

"Burn another one!" Big Mole sit up with a sarong tied up to her tiny pointy breast. "Burn another one means how much? Do you know . . . ! What happen if we have no money to pay the rent?"

"Kwang will help us . . . ! Burn another one first!"

The next-door neighbor knock against the plank wall.

"Hey! Stop talking so loud! So late . . . !"

Then Big Mole reluctantly burn another coil under Sachee's bed. Normally it takes two to last a whole night. Two at a time means four and is twenty cents a night. Every penny adds up in her mind. The rent is twenty dollars a month. Although the place is small, it has a kitchen and a place for friends to sit on boxes. It was home she never had before and love it.

She crouch on her canvas bed, just watching aimlessly at the coil shooting out its spot of light in the darkness. And out of this spot of light she saw a vision of Yeow, smiling when he wanted something. She begin to see herself trap with no self-esteem underneath him. It force her to look deeper within herself, she saw herself full of self-pity, no guts, like Ah Seow. Her mind start to expand under the spot of light. She think about Kwang. His interest and his generosity that has no string attached, the twinkle in his eyes when he grin. It make her wonder and compare herself with Kim, something she never thought of before.

As the coil burn further it leave behind a semicircle of suspended ashes and break off. The fall of ash cut off her trend of thoughts. She look at Sachee. He was snoring like laughing. Big Mole frown and stood up to push him over to sleep on one side, to stop the snoring and the laughing look.

The still night hides nothing. Everything is revealed. Even the screeching insects outside sound louder. The tapping hands and feet of the small gray wall lizards, eating mosquitoes on the atap roof, give away their positions. The occasional sounds of their hollow chirping through their glands seem to speak a special language as they call on others to mate.

In the heat of this humid night Big Mole sits on her bed and wish her grape-size mole can disappear, her breasts bigger. She slip back into her thin blanket and touch herself, touch her body. Then with lizards clicking in sweaty darkness, she masturbate for the very first time.

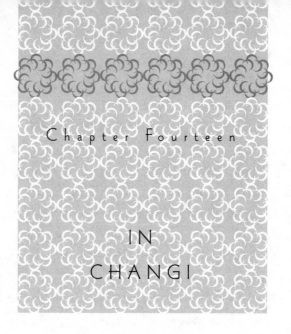

Although Ah Paw's death remain a mystery for the adults to gossip about, it makes no difference to Kwang's boys anymore. The heat of the spider games is at its peak. All the hard-core spider boys in Singapore, rich from the coin scrambling on ghost nights, are matching among themselves for three spiders to represent each district in their Olympic Games, this year held at Redhill because the winner was from there last year.

Yeow was thinking about putting in appearance before the games or not. Timing was important. He pick up the phone and call Cigarette Woman to send him Chai who has started to run his Chinatown boys with a heavy hand.

Chai was broke and waiting for his overdue wages from Yeow. His hair was crew-cut due to the traditional hundred days' mourning period for his grandmother, Ah Paw. When Yeow's call came he bikes half the length of Singapore from Chinatown to see his boss in Katong.

The door of the beach house was open when Chai arrive and sweats into Yeow's lounge. A ceiling fan turned slowly above the coffee table with its tin of 555 brand cigarettes.

"Lots of traffic?" Yeow smile and sip his coffee coolly on the smooth leather couch.

"Crazy!" Chai fume about it and help himself to the smokes in the tin.

"I don't get you here for nothing." Yeow flick him a light with his Ronson. "Tell me, what is all this spider game stuff worth? I am very interested."

"You count it yourself . . . !" Chai puff out smoke. "Last year, thirty-two districts all front up thirty-two dollars for each spider they enter. Ninety-six spiders altogether . . . more than three grand for the champ to take all . . . !"

One is a bull, the other a wolf.

"That is a lot of water," the wolf smile about the money with a leg up on the knee to rub his toes. "Kwang will be fat if he can really win."

"Fat?" the bull's eyes roll up in his head. "Very fat . . . !"

"He will be grinning," the wolf agree. "What about his chances?"

"Nobody can guarantee," Chai admit. "But I will throw down my pants to punt all on him."

Yeow just smile and say nothing. It makes Chai wonder and ask, "Are you coming out, then?"

"Depends. . . . I am not sure yet. Why?"

"Come out . . . !" the bull suggest with a hand out. "Throw your weight on the sideline, the sideline betting is even bigger . . . !"

"How much are you talking?"

"Imagine it yourself. Last year the Redhill boys pull up a few hundred together. They laugh away with around ten grand . . . !"

"Ten grand . . . !" The wolf stop rubbing his toes in astonishment at the amount of turnover in these boys' games he has underestimated. "How many of those spider guys are there?" He need this further detail once he sense something really big.

"Six to seven hundred last year. More this year. Every year more areas want to join. This is not a small thing. . . ."

"I heard a big shot is running the show, familiar with him?"

"Familiar . . . ! Big fat old fellow, we call him Shoot Bird for his crossed eyes. He live in Changi, why?"

"He must be something. . . . Wonder how he started it?"

"He give away a spider gold medal worth two ounces."

"Waah . . . is that all . . . !"

"Is a fact!"

"Did he make any out of this?" Yeow snap his finger to mention money.

"No, no . . . he do it just for fun . . . ! Very loaded fellow."

"I feel like meeting him . . . just for a bit of handshake. No problem with you?" To rub shoulders with brilliance and make himself brilliant, like Cheong Pak say.

"Make it tomorrow round about twelve when the Changi market close."

"Why then?"

"Tomorrow all the spider heads have to front up their cash to register with him first. I know him well. He won't like to see any of us until tomorrow, to play fair."

"Fair enough." Yeow stand up for Chai to go. "I see you tomorrow at the same time, okay?" He can see his bull is desperate for money, but he wants to know his limits.

Chai is also an individual who take nobody's shit. But he feel low about asking for money. He rub his big nose with head down and patience running out, like about to breathe out fire. Then the quick wolf pull out three crispy hundred-dollar notes from his purse to water the fire.

"Don't be shy to ask," Yeow encourage him to make his authority clear, subtly without being offensive.

Then Chai admit about wages. "Yeow," movingly, "nice of you to say it out. Make me feel a lot easier. . . . I do that the next time."

"Don't forget, anyone can forget," Yeow said skillfully to tame his bull completely.

And so Chai bikes away happily with his bicycle bell ringing and Yeow waving with smiles before he walk to the beach. The more he walk, the more he think. He smile about powerful Ng Koo. She has already said to him a week ago on the bed after a screw, "Why don't you let me buy you a car? Then you can come and see me more often."

"What for? All I need is the fucking driver's license," he purposely swear. "Can't fucking read and write. . . . How to get it . . . !"

She love his heavy language which make her feel sexy all over. "That is not a problem," she said smoothly. "How many do you want?"

"What about the fucking police if I am caught?"

"The police is in my hand."

Thoughts travel faster than the speed of light and make time disappear. By this time Yeow has walk the whole length of Katong Beach. He sit down to watch the rainbow cast over the sea. And smile again at the immediate thought of meeting Kwang again after a gap of several months. But he found it hard to separate the angel face of Kim who also appear inside the scene. To switch her off he pick up small flat stones to throw like flying disks, bouncing on the coming waves.

Kim was feeling restless and went to visit Big Mole.

"Why don't you come and see me nowadays?" she ask Big Mole sitting on a box eating plain rice porridge alone.

"I am not like you," Big Mole scorn. "I have to worry about my rent. I have to move out . . . !"

"How much is your rent?"

"Twenty dollar a month . . ."

"That is not much. I lend it to you."

"How to pay you back?"

"Wait for Yeow to come home."

"Wait for what? Somebody said Chai has met with Yeow secretly, many times, more than a month ago! I am going to depend on myself from now on, even if I have to die!"

Kim squat down with disbelief.

"Are you sure about Yeow?"

"Very sure." Big Mole know how Kim feel and warn, "Sometimes Yeow is like a devil with many face. Don't waste time on him."

"How do you know that?" Kim retaliate. "You never said things like that before. Why you want to talk behind his back? That is not fair . . . !"

"Who do you trust, me or him?"

Unlike Kwang who always try to screw her, Yeow didn't even touch Kim when she give him the chance on that unforgettable romantic night together.

"I trust him more than you," she sour up and walk away.

Normally Big Mole will go after Kim over silly little things, to make up like good friends do after a bit of friction. But not this time. Time change people. Her guts has got bigger. She was determine to stand up for herself, even at a dead end. This dead end was like a door with no key out.

The only way was to take a risk and gamble. Through Sachee's and Ah Seow's new friendship, she knew a dollar can make from fifty to a hundred if the pool keep turning over all the way to win the grand final.

Her hope in Kwang to win was very strong. As a professional who spy on people for a living under Yeow, she has watch all kind of people. But she has never seen anybody as determine as Kwang. And she count out her last cent which add up to over five dollars to think about betting behind Kwang on spider day.

Kwang has developed a new way of feeding his spiders by tying up the tiny bedbug alive with hair dangling around a bamboo split. Every time his spiders pounce for it, he fish it away to play speed with them, make them smarter and quicker. When they caught it, he drags the hair on the bamboo for their jaws to bite their meals tighter, to become stronger and more aggressive. Some of his spiders can hang on to their meals with their jaws in midair.

In the knockout competition under the huge banyan, Kwang's spiders defeated everybody and win the right with three spiders to call all the shots. This happen even before he use his king, which he keep quiet about for strategic reasons. Ah Seow was delighted. "Like that, you sure to win," he say to boost the team spirit.

Sachee also join in and make himself useful.

"Big Brother," he address Kwang, "what do you want me to do? Just say. . . ."

Ah Seow pull him aside. "Don't worry about here, ask Big Mole to come and bet. A few dollar can make a lot. If we win, we can start fish business together." Ah Seow is responsible for working out the grand total of cash for pool betting on the sideline.

And Sachee speed away. Halfway home he saw her. "Big Mole . . . !" he cried out. "Where are you going?"

"Why?" Big Mole ask.

"Bet on Kwang . . . !" Sachee suggest quickly. "Maybe we don't have to move out, go nowhere . . . ! If win we don't have to worry about money anymore."

"I know," Big Mole said with thin lips tight. And they walk together to buy with her last money and savings ten dollars' worth of shares at ten cents each from Ah Seow and his best friend, San, the referees of the village who collect the cash and issue receipts.

That day they collect over five hundred dollars from a crowd of more than two hundred who have been saving up for their big occasion. Under the banyan, surrounded by his worshipers, Kwang was quiet with his arms fold all the way on a buttress trunk. There is a lot of things in his mind. What happens if I lose? His one-track thoughts are jolted by everybody looking at the money and at him with hopeful eyes. Those silent eyes is pressure and make him feel lonely. Big Mole, who is used to watching people, saw this from instinct.

"What are you going to do next?" she went over to Kwang and ask. To chat him down from pressure.

"I think . . . I think I go to Chinatown."

"Looking for Chai?"

"Ya, talk a bit and see if we are going together on his bicycle. I have to go to Changi tomorrow to put our village name down."

"Changi is very far away, have to change bus . . . how many time?"

"Three times." And they start to walk.

"If it is important, ten times is also never mind. . . . Why run after Chai just for a bicycle?"

"Only temporary. I buy my own bicycle if I win."

"If?" Big Mole stare with her money at risk.

"Ya," he grin about it. "If not, we lose everything."

"That hard," Big Mole bite her nail. "If so, what are you going to do then?"

"Think about it later. . . . No use thinking about losing."

"True. Are you going alone tomorrow?"

"Better like that. Everybody want to go, they will grumble if I choose anybody. I can only take two."

"Why don't you go with Kim?"

"She don't like what I do. . . . Can you ask her for me?"

"We just had a quarrel. . . ."

"Over what?" he ask quickly, before she finish.

"Is not important," Big Mole hold back the truth. "I go and ask her for you," with concern that he might explode at the wrong time and spoil all their hopes.

"Tell her we all go together, three of us," Kwang suggest before she go to the bamboo deck.

In Changi, the man nicknamed Shoot Bird at more than fifty years old is still as wealthy and as healthy as ever. He started the game in 1950 to promote his coffee shop when he saw poor boys with no toys to play catch the wrestling spider after the terrible time of the Japanese occupation. And his business grow like magic because crowds attract crowds. He now has many trucks hired out to hawkers and still owns the big corner coffee shop with more space outside for extra chairs and tables under two large shady trees.

On this spider registration day, which is a Saturday, all the tables outside were reserved with free cold drinks and light snacks for his spider heads arriving from as far away as Jurong at the other end of Singapore. Standing tall and proud with a big belly under the tree, he is a figure nobody who arrive can miss. They all shake his hand with love. After a brief handshake with Yeow who arrive with Chai, he ask Chai, "Where is that boy? Third last year. Is he out this year?" Meaning Kwang.

"No, he is in," Chai reply. "We are waiting for him."

"Should be here anytime soon," Yeow blend easily with the occasion where everybody knows everybody, except himself. He imagined that Shoot Bird was sizing him up sideways, but actually his crossed eyes were looking in the other direction.

This is where Kwang and the girls arrive, causing other heads to turn and wonder, why girls? Kwang wave at them all and said, "I see Shoot Bird first."

Shoot Bird just shakes his head because he remembers that Kwang was the one who start calling him by the nickname first, two years ago. Kim was angry at the sight of Yeow. She point a finger at him and said, "How come you are here?" With a hurting face.

"Join the fun," Yeow evade her and shake hand with Kwang. "I just come back! How are you?" he smile and ask at Kwang. "Big day tomorrow?"

"Ya, we talk later," Kwang grin without noticing Kim's face. He introduce the girls to Shoot Bird who is looking surprised at them.

"Are you all here for tomorrow?" Shoot Bird ask the girls.

"Yah, same team with me," Kwang reply for them.

There is no law against girls. In fact the big man enjoy the new excitement of something different. But he was mixed up about Yeow and Chai, who he thought were from Ho Swee Hill. "What district are you actually playing for?" he ask them.

Red with embarrassment, Yeow look at Chai. Chai stare at Big Mole. Big Mole look at Shoot Bird and Kwang. Then Yeow said, "We here for Chinatown." To stop the ugly situation with so many eyes staring and because he knew the Chinatown boys has not arrive.

When they do, cunning Yeow bought their spiders from them to represent Chinatown with Chai.

"Is the same thing, okay?" he said to them. "I pay for the entry fees. You can have the money if I win." To sweeten their faces and force them out of the way.

That year thirty-five districts pay thirty-five dollars on each spider to fund the winner's bonus. A maximum of thirty-five people per district to attend the games was also agreed. Too many people have gone out of control and caused fights before. Everyone with a participating spider was given a number and their district written on a bamboo chip. The day ended with a party given by Shoot Bird who show them all the gold medal. But Kim don't want to sit at the same table as Yeow and Chai. She becomes nice to Kwang again and sticks her tongue out at the other two before they go.

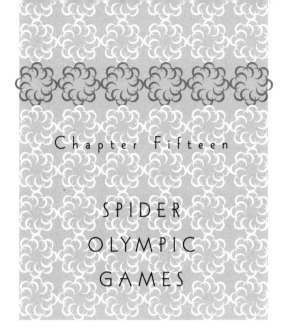

Chapter Fifteen

SPIDER OLYMPIC GAMES

It is the Sunday morning of the Spider Olympic Games. All the spider boys of Ho Swee Hill have been waiting before ten o'clock under the huge banyan in the playground. Including those who can't go, more than two hundred of them crowd around Kwang who squat down with spider box in his hand.

"Show you all something first before we go," he boast in a great mood. "Don't say I didn't let you all see my king first." And let it out to make his boys spell, "Woh!" at its prick, its size, its rich colors, powerful arms, legs, jaw, and tusk teeth.

"Let me show you how the king move," Kwang boast again and pass a selected hard-core boy another spider box. "Here, use this to kombang [compare] with my king and see how."

The other boy's spider was a big one too. Both spiders jump into the arena make for the occasion. They stare at each other and start to war dance floatingly. When they flipper arms and lock jaw, Kwang's toss the other in midair an inch away with one flip of both arms. Then the other tumble up to regain its posture and bull charge to ram back. Kwang's toss it away for another tumble, again and again like a cat playing with a mouse.

"Show to win or not?" Kwang glee. "Enough?" And snap his finger at it. It look up, he turn a back hand at it. It leap onto his back hand and wait like a cat. So well train with all the love, cares, and patience! The spider and his master once more spell amazement on every hard-core spider boy's face.

And the master with his pride swelling like to leave the best till last. He declare proudly with his king on his back hand, "This year I sure to win. If not, I chop off my head . . . ! I tell you all why."

Before Kwang answer his own question, Ah Seow slap on his back.

"Hey . . . ! Hey . . . ! Your mother behind you!"

Yee has heard rumors and meaning to check him up for a long time. She appear from behind the old banyan.

Ah Seow's words is like thunderbolt that change Kwang's face pale with no time to box up his king. In the split second his king appear to be looking up at him, he also look up and saw Yee's cane coming down. He bend to protect his spider and took the lash on his back, then run with the king inside both hands cupping together like a person running with handcuffs on.

Yee screams like a madwoman after him. "This time I am going to kill you! I have no more eyes to see!" Thinking he is still a little kid like parents sometimes often do.

Although Kwang can run faster, it was not easy to run with hands cuffed by spider inside. Their speed was evenly match. Though his stamina was good, when a person is mad, stamina is better.

He lost his nerve at the only person in the world who can scare him more than hell, ran uphill, and slip with nothing to hold. He roll down with spider firmly cupped inside. The moment he landed, he look to check and saw one of its arms squashed by his own hands. And quickly box it up.

When his mother caught up he grab her cane and whip her back like mad.

"Go and die! Go and die! I am not your son anymore!" And walk away at the youth age of fourteen.

It was not the physical pain. It was the words that break Yee's heart into pieces. And she fainted. Villagers rub white flower oil on her nose to revive and console her. "Let him go . . . ! Let him go . . . !" they say.

"The world nowadays is turning the other way. . . . His feather has grown . . . !"

The place Kwang go to was the farmer patch by the big yam leaves where all his spiders drink the morning dew. His grief over his injured spider is unbearable. An arm was crush and twisted. He howls it out to relieve himself with nobody around.

Ah Seow, who knew where he go, together with San, Big Mole, and Kim, found him squatting with chin on the spider box.

"Get lost!" he flare up at the sight of them.

Ah Seow startles backward with record books and other spider boxes clonking inside his shoulder bag. But not Big Mole who has become bold.

"Get angry with us is no use," she said. "What are you going to do now?"

"Hard to say," Kwang look away and mumble. "Have to find a place to stay. I think my prick mother will take my two small brothers away."

"I think so too," Kim admit quietly.

"Then what to do?"

Big Mole continue. "I have ask Sachee to follow them."

"Ya," Ah Seow confirm.

"Don't worry," San assure with his calm face. "I know my father will find something for them and your mother. We will find them no matter where they go, we are surrounded by friends . . . !" And give Kwang the best peace of mind in crisis time.

Their words wake him up. "Ya," he whisper and stand up. "Stay here all day also no use."

"Let me look at your spider." Kim took the box from him.

At first they all thought his spider is dead. And they all look. They saw the spider biting at the injured arm and shakes it off like disconnecting a joint. It look a lot better already. Ah Seow whisper aloud to San, "Spider with one arm can still fight . . . !" Which is true, all of them do. They normally take a day or two to recover and can grow a new arm in a few month or so.

"No need to prick talk, lah," Kwang grumble and snap his finger at it. The spider look up. He gently spit saliva for it to drink. Then box it up with a female inside and said to San, "We better go down and divide the pool money back to everybody. I don't want to go to Redhill. We can't win now."

But when they went down all his waiting boys insist he should go. Some says, "We wouldn't regret . . . ! Die, die together . . . !" Others said, "Maybe we can still win with the other two, give it a go . . . ! Better to die fighting than nothing!" Another say, "Stupid not to go when you pay the entry fees . . . !"

"They are right, don't waste time," said San, who know how to say the right word at the right time. "Your two small brother is alright with my father now."

"And Sachee is there . . . !" Big Mole assure further.

"Ya . . . !" Kim pull him up. "You must go . . . !"

The sense of participation becomes powerful. It wash away personal grief and change Kwang. "Ya, lah," he finally admit like born again. "No point running away. . . . We can play smart to win at least some money back. I think I know who else can win. . . .

"We go," he grin. "And die, die together!"

"Ya . . . !" And "Ya, lah . . . ! Die, die together!" All his spider boys from big to small throw up their hands to support him.

The Olympic Games start at 1:00 P.M. The selected party of thirty-five was cheer off by the rest at the foot of Ho Swee Hill. And they climb the highest hill toward Redhill and then over other hills, eastward like an adventurous trip. Some of them armed with slingshots shoot down wild fruits and some unlucky birds. Flying lizards were also their targets on their way.

After an hour of bush tramping they come on top of the red cliff of Redhill which has a large space below reserved for a brick factory. They look down at trucks unloading planks and bottle crates to stage seats around five spider arenas, planted far apart in the shade which draws a straight line from the sun crossing west over the cliff.

Before the team go down they discuss tactics. San ponder and ask, "Who else you think is good? We should prepare something behind them."

"I know," Kwang said decisively with a plan in his mind. "Use half our pool money to roll behind the guy from Bukit Timah, crew-cut hair like Sachee. Spread out just a little bit on ourself first. Save the rest to see what happen."

"That is the best way," Ah Seow said beside Big Mole. "Spread our capital out." And he lead the way down the slope.

By the time they all went down, another truck has arrive with cases of soft drinks provided by the generous Shoot Bird who lives for the annual affair. Spider boys who get a lift in from the main road hop out to help unload the drinks. Two of them were Yeow and Chai. Kim and Big Mole pretend they didn't see them. Yeow don't mind, he just smile inside with his own thoughts that is beyond them.

"Hey . . . ! Monkey Boy!" Chai look at Kwang. "What happen to your eyes? So swollen . . . !"

"Waste that kind of talking later," Kwang growl at Chai. "What do you want to find out?"

"Don't get us wrong," Yeow smile. "I am only here to join the fun, come to see you win. What are you going to do after this?"

"Don't know, see what happen first."

"We are only bluffing around here for Chinatown," Chai make it clear. "I am throwing my pants behind you beforehand. Alright with you?"

"A word is a word," Yeow back it up. "Make it this way. Half of the win is yours, loss not your problem. Fair?"

"No point talking now," Kwang said straight. "I better show you what happen to my best one today." And open his box.

"That is like dead . . . !" Chai wince and look mute at Yeow.

"You are right," Yeow said to Kwang. "No point talking now." And walk away with disappointment inside.

Chai block Yeow's path and plead. "Yeow, you have register a spider. You have to play . . . ! Where are you going? I recommend you here! Don't make me lose face."

"I know . . . ! Okay!" Yeow snarl quietly like trapped in a sticky web by Chai's advice. And turn around to watch Kwang walking with his crew to join other familiar groups smelling each other out, drinking free drinks as they chat.

Yeow saw that Kwang was very popular and decided to stay.

"Why not?" was the reason he gave Chai.

The last truck to arrive was Shoot Bird and those previous Olympic champions who will referee the games. The crowd claps to welcome them. They all had a gold chain with the spider gold medal dangling on their unbuttoned chests. Many hard-cores, including Kwang, walk over to shake their hands. And Yeow photograph each of them in his head, including those who shake their hands.

He ask Chai, "Do you know them?"

"Ya, every single one," Chai reply.

Beaming Shoot Bird had the Olympic gold medal hanging on his fat chest topped by a laughing Buddha face. He initiates the opening ceremony by climbing on the back of his truck with a hailer and blast, "Tew chiam! Tew chiam!" to pair the players by drawing lots.

"One against Two on table one! Five against Six on table five!" And so on.

For the preliminary rounds in the five separate arenas, a one-square-foot white board was sitting on a crate. Behind are rows of planks on more crates for seats at different levels by turning the length and breadth of the crates around in three different ways. Viewing the match was like looking down into a pit.

When the referees are ready they take their seats on red bricks. The referees let their spiders jump on the arena and cup them separately under transparent glass cups for public display. They give the bettors five minutes to look, ten minutes to work out their bets and hand them to them against receipts for safekeeping. And earn 2 percent on the turnover money.

For the first preliminary between ten spiders nobody from Ho Swee Hill was in yet. But Bukit Timah was and make money for Kwang's team betting behind him.

Later Big Mole's spider was knocked out, but Kim win. Kwang's one-armed spider stunned the crowd with a shock success. It just keep dancing floatingly backward for a good thirty seconds before it knock out the confused opponent. Even Kwang was surprised at the miracle recovery. He knew the longer the spider dance, the better the form.

The punting on the sideline was conservative in the first preliminaries, slightly better in the second round. Kwang and Bukit Timah continue to win their way into the quarterfinals where money change hands faster and bigger.

Every moment becomes more exciting. Auction noises for public bets sent the bookkeepers running up and down the five tables separated at twenty meters apart. Betting is also a race with time. San arrive behind Kwang and said, "We have turn over nearly two thousand all together. How now?"

"Not quite so sure about myself yet, play smart safe first."

Kwang decide quickly. "Use one third on me, two on Bukit Timah." For San to carry the order back before the hot favorite from Bukit Timah is booked out.

They win on both sides again to double the money. Kwang feel like almost kissing his spider to death. The big crowd give his one-arm king a standing ovation.

"Who else is winning?" He turn round to Ah Seow who rush back from checking other result.

Ah Seow said hastily, "Bedok, Geylang, Ponggol, and Jurong."

A spy add, "Chai and Yeow is rolling behind Jurong."

Another said, "They are lending out money, too."

"That is their problem," Big Mole advise behind Kwang. "Concentrate on ourself first."

Because by spider law all the winning players have to stick to their seat, Kwang was feeling frustrated. He turn around and ask, "Where is San?"

"Right behind you," said San, the supercoordinator. "We are rising to three thousand.... How about half-half between us and Bukit Timah?"

"Why not . . . !" Kim answer for Kwang.

"Ya, okay," Kwang confirm with a nervous grin. He could see his spider is exhausted and thirsty under the transparent glass cup on the white board for public display, but is not allow to drink by spider law.

In the semifinal which left eight spiders to match on four separate tables, the biggest crowd gathered was on Jurong against Bukit Timah. It was like the clash of the giants. More than half of the total spider boys pack around them with barely any chance to glimpse at the action.

"Money lost is another thing," moans those with no seats who are standing. "We don't even have a chance to watch . . . !"

But not Yeow and Chai who are the spider players of the day, among the privileged on the front row betting behind Jurong.

"I hope you are right," Yeow said to Chai just before the referee rings the bell. And they win again. Bukit Timah lost. Ah Seow almost fainted at the size of the loss. It was fifteen hundred dollars. But Kwang win his way into the final to recover the money. He was so ecstatic he hear nothing when San report the Bukit Timah loss into his ear drown by all the applause.

After the noise die down, San repeat, "Bedok, Ponggol, and Jurong is on the final. Bukit Timah out."

"I thought Bukit Timah is better than Jurong," Kwang mumble grinningly and ask, "How many rounds?"

"Eight, according to Ah Seow."

"Any injuries on Jurong?"

San look to a spy. The spy said, "Lost a leg."

"That is not much. What about Bedok and Ponggol?"

"Ponggol nothing. Hot favorite now."

"That tough. . . . Anyway, how Bukit Timah lost to Jurong?"

"Jurong bites like a dirty dog," spy report. "Left Bukit Timah with no arms and ran."

"I hope Jurong is not a bulldog spider," Kwang guess. "Better to see who face who before we bet."

Big Mole, who watch things quietly, said, "No time to wait . . . !"

Then Ah Seow suggest, "What about don't be greedy? Throw two grand in, save one up for the grand final? Just in case we lose?"

But the majority in one voice said, "No . . . ! One way all the way!" And it was agreed to throw everything behind Kwang.

Yeow and Chai was winning so much money by sticking with Jurong on the same table they have forgotten about Kwang until the name was announce by Shoot Bird with the hailer. Chai stop counting his cash and look at his boss doing the same thing.

"Yeow!" he said. "You hear what Shoot Bird say? Is hard to believe. . . . Kwang is in!"

"I am not deaf," Yeow said warily. "Funny thing, he must have lives like cat. . . . What about change side to roll behind him?"

"No, never bend backward...!" Chai insist. "Jurong is a bulldog spider. Kwang will lose even if he have two arms...!"

"Alright, alright, stick to the same course. No point arguing anyway what I don't know. Let's see what the dice say." Yeow watch Shoot Bird about to draw lots on the truck to match up the four finalists.

Smiling Shoot Bird is a man who take pride in his organizing ability like hobby and is quite a joker. He pause with the hailer to quiet down the buzzing crowd. And announce dramatically, "The final on table five...is...! Bedok against...Jurong! Table two...is...! Ho Swee Hill! Against Ponggol!" Like show business, making a thousand voices roar and roar with hands punching up behind their team and echoes bouncing back from the red cliffs.

Kwang just keep staring and mind-talks with his pet before the match start. Like the way he do every morning during training. And by the magic of such bondage, or skill, he win in seven rounds to enter the grand final. Ah Seow almost fall into a trance because of happiness when he saw the cash come flowing back. It was double, to nearly six grand. Even the girls were jumping with delight, the whole team was ecstatic.

On the other side, between Bedok and Jurong, Jurong was also winning like the swiftest horse on the track. In four rounds his opponent ran away with no arms left. And like Chai, all the great punters good at picking winners were a hundred percent behind Jurong. The odds on the favorite is two to one in Jurong's favor on the betting list, with the cash held by the five referees. Which total more than thirty thousand dollars from a thousand gamblers representing the many others who wait at home.

A loud alarm clock was placed in the arena with the time set for 3:00 P.M. All the gear from the other stages were use to make one big stage for as many as possible to glimpse the action. The seats was marked with chalk and numbered to stop confusions and eruptions. Then Shoot Bird proudly walk with his five referees to take their seats on bricks beside the two finalists, who don't care about anything but just staring at their beloved spiders caged under two cups in the arena. Talking inside quietly to them, like farmer and his dog.

At five to three the chief referee ring a brass bell and call out, "Five minutes left!" for the privileged with numbered tickets to take their correct seats. And the rest scramble to stand behind, just to smell the occasion. Although there is no chance to actually see the action, some even climb up the cliffs to get a complete bird's eye, not at the spiders because they are so small, but at the people.

When the alarm clock ring at 3:00 P.M. the serious chief referee stand up and shout, "Start!" with a symbolic hand-chop above the two glass cups caging the spiders on the arena. And lift them up for the two gladiators to come out.

Although one has no left arm, the other limping on only five instead of six legs, and even though tired out, when they meet they war dance for a record of over thirty seconds before they jump at each other. It is Jurong that takes the first leap with jaws aimed at Kwang's arm. Wrestling spiders are hot-tempered creatures. Once they clash, they keep clashing from crawling to standing positions with everything they have. Stabbing, biting, boxing, wrestling, pushing. Then crumbled up like a ball, and flung apart. The referee shout, "One round!"

In round nine the tip of Kwang's right arm was caught by the powerful jaws of Jurong. Kwang shakes and shakes until the end of the joint snap off. And Jurong falls back with the tip still in its mouth!

Kwang leap up to smash head down at Jurong's mouth, knocking a tusk and some teeth off. Then they start to bang heads like bulls, crazy with injuries, closer and closer to the edge of the block.

The crowd shout, "Record! Record!" for the tenth round.

By this time Jurong with smashed jaws and less legs starts to wobble against the strong legs of Kwang whose head is more solid though its arm is almost paralyzed. It keep pushing until Jurong reach the edge. Then Kwang use its remaining strength to push Jurong over the edge of the white block, down the cliff of the bottle crate, falling.

And the crowd kick down the stadium in their rush to get a look.

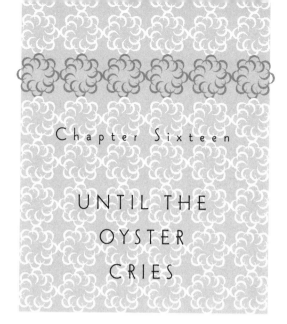

Chapter Sixteen

UNTIL THE OYSTER CRIES

Kwang came back from Redhill to discover his mother has quit her job after popular Wong has promised to help her set up a food stall near the temple.

"That is not all bad," Big Mole cheer him up at her place. "At least your two brother is not somewhere else we don't know!"

"We all of us will look after them even if you are not around," promise one of the main spider boys near the kitchen. "We are rich now because of you...!"

"Where are you going to stay?" Kim ask

Kwang. His clothing is in a shoulder bag and has been salvaged by Sachee after his mother has thrown it out.

"Stay with us . . . !" interrupts Sachee fiercely, fanning the fire at the clay stove with Ah Seow helping to boil the water for coffee. "Just buy a canvas bed! Right or not?" he ask Ah Seow.

"Not now," reply Ah Seow, adding more wood in the stove. "The canvas bed shop has just closed."

"I have a spare bed at home," says pleasant-face San, sitting on a box opposite Kwang. "I can get it now, if you want."

"Ya, okay for temporary," Kwang agree with mixed feeling. "Tomorrow I will buy a bicycle in Chinatown, look around for a new place."

Yeow who appear again in Chinatown with Chai was pondering his next move on Kwang privately in the early evening.

"We only lost by half a nose . . . !" Chai mourn the heavy defeat.

"I lost five times more than you, so don't grumble about it, okay?" Yeow shut him up. He saw the loss as a blessing in disguise. After a meal in Yeow's favorite coffee shop they catch a taxi to Ho Swee Hill.

"Come to my place first or what?" Chai ask when near his house on the pitch-black night.

"No, I see you later." Yeow took the torch. "I have to check how Big Mole and Sachee monkey around myself."

On his way past the kids' playing space in front of Kwang's house, below the bamboo deck, he stop at the sight of Kim cleaning the table alone after her tall strong father has eaten and retire to read picture comics in his room. Yeow switch off his torch to watch her closer below the dark side of the deck. The glow from the kerosene lamp reflecting on her long hair swept to one side make her face even more beautiful. He cough to catch her reaction.

She look out.

"Who is that?"

"Just me." Yeow lean on the railing. "Come to see you and Kwang. I come up?"

"Huh, so it's you," she say sarcastically with her hands on hips. "I thought you are not talking to me again. . . . You better not come up. Kwang is not living here anymore." Looking pissed off outwardly and yet somehow is not inside. She feels somewhere in between.

"How come . . . !" he shocks up quietly. "I . . . I don't understand."

"And I don't want to waste time talking to you," she sneer with full lips tight. "Go and see Big Mole and find out for yourself."

"I am not going unless you tell me why," Yeow insist playfully, to make her talk further.

But fire is her nature. She took it as an offense.

"Do you want me to call my father out?" she spit back impulsively.

"Shssh . . . ! Okay, okay," he back off with a hand up. "I'm going, I'm going." And trips on a fresh mango skin left there by the kids, stumbling backwards with left hand holding the torch up, right pressing down on the ground to prevent a total fall.

Kim felt straightaway sorry and rush out with the kerosene lamp from the table. Yeow limps up to her painfully.

"Have you hurt your leg?"

"No, just twisted the ankle a bit. Sprained my hand, that's all." Holding it with the torch under his armpit as Kim help him up three flights to the deck.

"I have some sprain medicine inside. You better stay here awhile."

"What about your father! All right with him?"

"My father is not a busybody." Kim go into her room to get a bottle of herbal lotion. "This stuff is very good, made by Kwang's Kung Fu father a long time ago."

She squats down. Yeow takes off his shoe to rub the ankle and let her massage his wrist.

"Hey Kim," he smile. "If you don't mind my asking, what about Kwang now? Do you have quarrels, or what?"

"No, it is not like that. His mother is back." She tells the whole story of the day briefly. And bites off the bandage cloth.

"That is sad, very sad. . . . Where is she now?"

"At neighbor's place with his two little brothers."

"And your own brother?" Meaning Ah Seow.

"At Big Mole's with Kwang. They all there."

"Kwang can't stay forever," he digs further. "That place is too small. . . . It is not a good move. I can give him a hand."

"Just there for tonight. He is looking for a new place tomorrow."

"I better see him. Let's go together, okay?"

Kim make her excuse after a second thought.

"No, you go yourself. I have other things to do."

The invisible screen about Yeow is still strong for her due to what Big Mole said. But the moment he disappear in the dark she starts to wonder the whys that make her heart so high. Thinking about his fall on the mango skin which somehow remind her of falling overboard at Clifford Pier. And laugh as she washes the dishes.

* * *

The night was still young at Big Mole's place. An eating and drinking party was going on to celebrate the spider victory. The place was packed inside and out, even the tiny kitchen where half-drunk older boys are drinking rice wine in small teacups.

"One more cup! One more cup!" they insist to Sachee who has suggested the wine and is already drunk, smoking and talking big about pet fish business.

"Okay, alright," Sachee big talk tipsily. "Let's see who can drink more . . . !" And bottom up the wine in one go.

"Tell my Big Brother to do the same!" He indicate Kwang who is already flat out with a fair amount inside, dozing on Sachee's bed with Big Mole tidying up the tiny space, herself quite drunk but feeling great at the outcome of the day that save her from the landlord.

Ah Seow was the only sober one, trying to hang around Big Mole.

"No use drinking too much," he advise her.

"What do you know?" she turn on him. "Once in a while is okay."

Yeow who arrive just then to find Kwang can't believe the whole scene in front of him. There was hardly room for him to get inside so at first he watched them through the window. The moment he tried to squeeze in to look for Big Mole, Sachee who is drunk and not very happy with him appear from nowhere and shoo him out.

"Hey! What are you doing here?" Sachee jumbles the words out. "This party is for Ho Swee Hill, not for Chinatown . . . ! Are you trying to spy around? Get out!" he burp. "Get out! Big Mole and me is not going to depend on you anymore. We want to do business ourselves!" He trip over a body on the floor. "Go! This is not your place!"

Yeow knew small Sachee too well to be offended. He ignore him and squeeze into the bedroom to see Big Mole. But other drunken spider boys agree with Sachee, block his way and say, "You better go back to Chinatown. This is not your territory. Get out!"

Yeow didn't take them seriously. "Just make sure you all don't burn down the house," he warn and smother the fire on the wood stove with the boiling pot of water nearly dried out. He see no reason to get mad.

It was more than a mile to Chai's place and the cold wind was blowing on the cloudy might. Yeow walk faster, but can't beat the rain at midway. He ran to the nearest place which is Kim's place and dash up the bamboo deck.

"Kim . . . ! Kim!" he call out.

Kim was folding the day's washing on her bed and came out at once at the sound of his voice.

"Is you again," she sigh. "You are a thick skin . . . ! What do you want now?"

Flexibility is Yeow's resource. The rain was pounding on the atap roof. "Look at the rain," he point up as it whip his wet face. "Is it possible to borrow an umbrella? Just a small favor. If you don't mind."

"How are you going to give it back? My father has to use it in the morning to get to work if it rain again."

"I go to Chai's place to borrow another one, give you back yours right away, okay?"

She look hard at him with hands on hips.

"And how are you going to hold the torch with that bad hand and hold the umbrella with the other one all the way there at the same time?"

"You are right, you are right," he admit smilely and squat down to look up at her. "Either I wait here awhile, or . . ."

"Or what?" she press further, scowling down at him.

He gesture helpless up at her. "What about help me with the umbrella to Chai's place . . . Just a ten-minute walk or so. Please?"

She agree to carry the umbrella to shelter him in the rain.

One incident leads to another from the twist of change. The wind was splashing through the growing rain. They huddle closer together against the storm. Their bodies keep rubbing together as they walk. Everything was automatic . . . the friction, the vibrations, the rhythm, the sensation. It just happen from the point of nowhere to somewhere, where the mind could say "no" no more.

It was so smooth. They don't even talk or look to make the moves. The howling storm was so fierce it join everything together. It tears the branches of the umbrella apart. And soaks them to the skin with not a soul around as they approach Chai's house which is not far from the playground under the huge banyan. They shelter there by the hollow with the small shrine of Grandfather God, Da Bo Gong. And kiss, kiss to warm the lips. Until she push up her fresh pointed mango breasts into his face, he smells smells and sucks sucks them under her big wet braless T-shirt. And the thunder roars with lightning in the dark night. And she spreads her legs apart across the huge buttress trunk, and yank off her underpant to massage herself with one hand, unzipping his pants down with the other, and pull him down on her. And grab her hands behind his naked bottom to force his front into her oyster, purring with her full lips wide as she control the rhythm as he move. Moving according to her wish. Until her oyster cry. To say "Yes!" to life. With tears in her almond eyes.

Then the thunder flash another powerful roar. Yeow glance at the shrine with fright. And hold her tight until the storm dies.

"Do you love me?" she ask tenderly.

"Yes, yes. Always," he admit nervously. "But what about Kwang...? Do you for him?"

"Sometimes, yes. Sometimes no."

And they agree to keep their secret to themselves.

When the storm died the party at Big Mole's place is also over with everybody going home, mainly because Sachee the big talker is knocked out by too much rice wine.

Kwang the hero of the occasion who drink for the hell of it is also still sleeping from the overdose he is not good at. His canvas bed is squeezed in the middle of the tight space used for walking in between Big Mole and Sachee's bed, just enough space for it to fit in. Exactly like a king-size bed, they join together.

By the time Big Mole is ready to sleep after cleaning up the party mess she had second thoughts about switching off the kerosene lamp against the wall above her. She look hard at Kwang sleeping sideways with his back facing Sachee, front facing her. Kwang sleeps with shorts and no shirt on as usual, pillowing on his shoulder bag with his clothing still inside. Although raised in brothels from childhood where she has seen countless naked men of all shapes and sizes and had tangles with street boys who try to rape her, it was a total new experience for Big Mole to be so close to somebody she respect more than anyone else. Though respect is not physical, but spiritual. She want to be touch, especially when the night is cold after rain and with no mosquitoes to disturb her thoughts. After looking at Kwang for quite some time, she move about to make squeaky noise on her bed to see if he will wake up. Then she lean over him to push snoring Sachee sideways. Purposely to wake Kwang up indirectly, without being obvious for what she need.

He wake up sleepily.

"Don't you feel cold?" she ask as an excuse.

"Ya, just a bit. But never mind," he mumble with eyes half closed.

"You want to share my blanket?"

"Ya, okay," he reply without concern.

And Big Mole cuddle closer to share her blanket as Kwang go back to sleep.

When the cock crows for morning to dawn it means the day is fine. Kwang waste no time to climb up to the farmer plot at mid-hill for his spiders to drink the morning dew. He contemplate them for a long time before he decide to free his beloved King, together with a few females. And bury some of his thick cash in a tin.

On his way down past the playground he call in at Chai's place.

"I heard Yeow is here with you. Where is he now?" he ask Chai sitting on the bench outside the gambling den. "I heard from boys he look for me."

"Didn't you see him?" Chai smoke. "He told me he is going to look for you at Big Mole's place. I am still waiting here for him, he must have used the temple way."

"I just came down from the hill. And you, what about you now? Come back to live here, or what?"

"No, no, can't be bothered with my old man now, he is cranking over my head like mad. Too many pipes of the black stuff. Can't handle to be around here anymore. I'm packing up. . . . You? I heard your old mother hen has broken off with you?"

"Ya, nearly kill everything for me at Redhill."

"At least you are fat from yesterday. What's the score?"

"Enough," Kwang reply modestly.

"I am giving up the spider business, what about you?"

"Thinking about it. Have to do something different. . . ."

"That's the way! Good for you."

"I am looking for a new place, to get away from here."

"Then we are on the same boat!" Chai feels very give face to Kwang. "Why not join me at Cheong Pak's place? He's a good old fellow, you are sure to like him."

"I don't like his wife, that cigarette woman."

"That's easy, just ignore her. Nothing to do with her. Yeow is in control. He always talk highly of you. He likes you. Let's brother on the same boat together."

"Ya, maybe for temporary." Kwang stand up. "I talk to Kim about it first."

"Na, be a man! Girls around cannot do anything much. Sit down first, for old time's sake. Here, have a smoke and wait for Yeow."

And Kwang sit down to smoke for the first time.

Big Mole and Sachee were eating breakfast when Yeow arrive.

"Big Mole." He squat with arms folded in front of them. "How are you now?" He has his reasons for trying to be nice.

"Alright." She eat with her head down. "Not too bad."

He watches her carefully. "I came to ask you just one thing. . . . Are you going to come with me to Chinatown, or fly away here by yourself? Just let me know, okay?"

"I don't know what you mean."

"Don't fool around with me, okay?"

"Okay."

"Tell me . . . what is happening here when I am not around?"

"I am not your slave!" she exclaim with a shiver of fire inside.

"Okay, okay. Do you know who own this place for you?"

Big Mole refuse to answer. And keep eating.

"All I want is answers. Fair?" Yeow light up a smoke.

Big Mole keep her head down and go on eating stubbornly.

He press harder. "Are you dumb, or what?"

She glance at Sachee, who smack down his chopstick. "You expect us to vomit?" the small boy exclaim. And stand up with fists bunched at four feet tall.

Sachee in a way is a mirror reflection of Yeow himself. He laugh inside at the little guy and stub out his cigarette before turning back to her. "Very well, Big Mole," he say, gesturing with his finger. "I won't bother you anymore. But just remember one thing. If you need help, don't be afraid to ask . . . okay?" And walk away, leaving a fine line behind.

The moment he is gone, Big Mole turn to Sachee. "We have to look after ourselves, better follow him."

Yeow is going to buy a new umbrella for Kim from the local shop. That morning Ah Seow was at school and Kwang's little brothers was out somewhere with their mother. Kim was sick in bed with a bad cold but she sigh with relief at the sight of Yeow. They kiss with even more passion in spite of her flu. Sachee knows his trade well. He doesn't climb up the creaky bamboo deck to peep between the gaps, he sneak behind the back of the house to do his job, to the windows where Kwang and Ah Seow used to jump out in the early days to train their spiders at mid-hill when Kwang's mother was at home. And not just that. He also has the patience to follow Yeow all the way out of the deck to meet Kwang and Chai at the gambling den. And he report back to Big Mole that they finally catch a taxi, outside of No Nose Bridge.

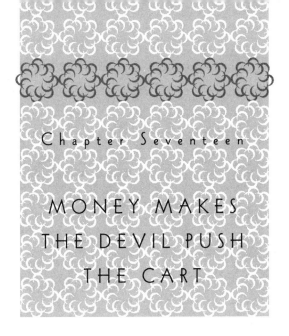

Chapter Seventeen

MONEY MAKES THE DEVIL PUSH THE CART

Big Mole was chopping firewood with her sarong tied up above her skinny breasts. She found it hard to believe what Sachee said he saw happen between Kim and Yeow.

"We must tell Kwang at once!" Sachee kick at the chopping block.

"No! We must look after ourselves first!" She strikes the ax on the block. "Why drum up trouble for ourselves!"

She knows she has to play Yeow's game in order to survive. He is like a smiling tiger who will punish them by isolating them, just like he does to any of his boys who rebel against his slightest whim. It makes her even more determined to be independent.

She hits the block with so much force her robe falls away from her breasts.

"How so?" ask Sachee, quietened down by her rare fury.

"Yeow can destroy people with no blood seen." She retied her sarong. "Better to pretend we don't know anything."

"What to scare . . . ? We tell Kwang first, he not scare of Yeow. He is on our side!"

"Nobody is on our side. I think Kwang is going to Chinatown, live with Yeow and Chai. He didn't leave anything behind."

"What about Kim?"

"Same thing, play dumb. But I will try to be nice to Ah Seow, he still has a lot of money. I think he likes me. So you must not laugh at me if I am nice back to him, you agree?"

"Ah Seow likes you?"

"Maybe. . . . Why not? He has tried once on me already. I will use his money to start fish business with him. . . . We have to be smarter now, you understand what I mean?"

"Ya, ya." Sachee nod with mouth shut tight. "Smarter than anybody first, right?"

"We go to Chinatown now. . . . We still have a lot of friends there who don't like Yeow quietly, see what they say behind his back. I also want to buy clothing for myself to look nicer for everyone, you agree?"

"Sure!" excited Sachee collect up Big Mole's firewood for the kitchen. Like little boy who is also fierce beyond his years, he dream of fighting fish. Then he think of smiling Ah Seow, and last of all his fiery hatred for the big dumb Chai.

On their way out of the village they meet San coming back from school, sucking a sugared shave ice ball.

"Sachee, Big Mole! Where you all going?"

"Chinatown," Big Mole reply before Sachee answer. "Going to the movies, haven't seen one for a long time. Come with us, lah?" Nice and persuasive, to make more friends and ensure survival.

"I have to go home and eat first, okay?"

"Is alright, we will wait for you."

"What about Ah Seow?" San ask. "We should all go together . . . ?"

"Ya, good idea," Big Mole agree with new cunning.

In Chinatown she is nicer to San than to Ah Seow. She even sit between San and Sachee in the movies, separated from Ah Seow, because she know that he would like to hold her hand. Like his parents, Ah Seow start to love at very young age. He is jealous inside but careful not to show it.

The changes in Big Mole make him feel even worse. Why was she buying clothes for a new image? She ask San, "What you think of this? And this? You like it? You think it will look nice on me?" All the time ignoring him.

She and San even talk about starting a pet fish shop for themselves. "Where do you think would be a good place?" she ask.

"Best to question my father first, he knows a lot of things like that. I can talk anything to him, same for you."

"That is a good idea. . . . He is a very nice man." She reminds San that his father is the only person in the village to help Kwang's mother start her business. And deliberately makes him proud of his father even more.

Casually she turn around to Ah Seow. "What about you . . . ?" she ask in offhand voice. "Do you dare to spend your money and join with us?"

"But that is what I always wanted to do!" Ah Seow jump in at the opportunity.

"Easier to talk than do," cunning Big Mole reply. "To do business needs big capital, how much you have to talk like that?"

"I make more than one thousand, from fifty dollars at the games!"

It is more money than Big Mole has all together and is what she wants although she feels she must also be honest with Ah Seow.

"Woh! You my boss with all that money! Buy more shares than I can!"

"More shares, less shares, it doesn't matter."

"If you agree, then, we work together?"

"I like that very much." Ah Seow try to catch her eye with special meaning.

"Shake hands first!" Sachee demand and stretch out his hand to seal the deal.

"Okay, lah." Ah Seow grab it.

"What about me?" Big Mole stretch out her thin brown arm.

Ah Seow grab Big Mole's hand even harder. "A word is a word!" He is so pleased with himself he forget to let it go.

"San, you be the witness," says Big Mole, taking back her hand.

"I witness for all of you," San promise. "And good luck too!"

"To all of us!" Big Mole laugh happily inside. "When can you talk to your father, lah?"

"Tomorrow, after school."

"Can I come too?"

"That is the way to do business!" San reply with a big heart.

San talks that night also to his mother, a warm-face woman who he knows must give the final nod. And Wong, the village calligrapher who writes letters for the illiterate villagers with relations still in China, says to his wife before they go to bed, "Well, Rice Woman, if you agree . . ." and waits for her approval.

"Then it is decided. . . . I will go all the way to give the three of them my hand."

The next sunny afternoon Wong clicks his abacus in front of the excited young entrepreneurs sitting on the cane settee in his simple office.

"Open your ears," he wags his finger at them. "To do business you must have a proper plan. First, remember to keep a smiling face for all your customers."

The three nod attentively.

"Who is going to keep the record book?"

Ah Seow raise his hand.

"Who is going to sit in front of the shop?"

Big Mole raise hers.

"Who is going to keep the money and buy the goods?"

Sachee shoot his hand up quickly but Big Mole smack it down immediately. "Is me," she smile, and ask, "But how to find the place to start?"

"I have an old friend with an empty shed next to his chicken-incubating shop in Geylang Serai. Tomorrow I will bring you all along for a chat with him. As for the fishes and tanks, I will look into another friend in Tua Payoh who breeds his own stock in the countryside to wholesale. Happy, everybody?"

"Yes, we are very happy. Thank you, Mr. Wong," Big Mole answer politely for all of them.

"Then don't waste my time! Come back tomorrow." He is due for opium smoking with the blind man who runs the Kuan Yin Temple with his ageless wife.

Geylang Serai is a mixed ethnic area with more Malays than Chinese. Indonesian Big Mole who look the same as Malay fit into the multiracial background perfectly. The Malays were curious because she could hardly speak their language. The Chinese were fascinated by her ability to speak Chinese like them. Fascination draws a crowd. Crowds attract more people. Their business prospers because of Big Mole being who she is.

With the help of Chai, Yeow manage to persuade Kwang to live at Cheong Pak's place. After tasting Kim, and with the powerful Ng Koo behind his secret affairs, Yeow's supreme personality starts to divide inside him. One day he takes Chai aside in Santeng, the breathing space of packed Chinatown, and says quietly, "You are the only one who know my place in Katong. Don't ever dare to drop in there without ringing me first, okay?"

"What's the big secret, Yeow?" Chai ask with his hands wide open. "Why not let it out between us . . . ?"

"Because you have a big mouth," Yeow snarl. "Do you expect me to tell you how long is my prick? Guess for yourself!"

"I don't get you," reply dumb Chai. "You mean you have some girls hanging around? I won't come over at all, if that's the case."

"That's better. . . . At least you know what I'm saying." He scowls to make sure that Chai remembers to keep away altogether from his love nest at the beach.

At Katong he waits constantly for Kim who often phones him. They spend more and more secret time together. Yeow pays for all her taxi fares. He teaches her to swim. He takes her to air-conditioned restaurants. They walk Katong Beach at sunset, go to the movies, make love in different ways in all the rooms. Their intoxicating time together seems to roll on endlessly, so that Kim doesn't want to go home and she sees less and less of Kwang.

Cheong Pak and his wife advise Yeow not to rush Kwang into anything.

"Pull your eyes longer to watch him first. Be patient with him," they say. "Money makes the devil push the cart. Let him waste all his money before we catch him."

Kwang has bought a new bicycle and is busy travel throughout Singapore to see the spider boys who glorify him as their hero. As Cheong Pak is expecting, his cash start to run out. To save face he ends up working on Shoot Bird's trucks as a laborer, delivering goods to the markets. At fifteen he is average height and slim, with muscles hard from all the lifting.

One day he drop over to Big Mole's fish shop to check up on his little brothers.

"Sit down first," Big Mole smile as she pull out the chair behind her at the counter. "Your little brothers are fine. How are you?"

"Not bad," he grin to make light of everything. "Still working hard for Shoot Bird."

"That why long time no see? How is Kim?"

"Don't know, hard to say. Kim don't like the place I stay.... Where is Sachee?"

"Out buying threadworms for the fishes."

"So how is business? And you yourself?"

"Good, very busy. Too far to come and go from Ho Swee Hill every day. Sachee and me have decided to move out, live somewhere around here in Geylang. Save a lot on bus fares."

"What about Ah Seow? Does he help much?"

"Only after school, and then what can he do? All he wants is to look at how much money we make."

"Always greedy for money! You should run the business yourselves."

"That's what I said to him the other day. He didn't like it and wanted to pull out his cash, tried to threaten me."

"Prickly bastard. So?"

"But you are right. I offered to buy him out."

"Did he agree?"

"Why not? He makes a good profit. He put out with a thousand and gets back five hundred more. What about yourself? Are you happy with your work? It must be hard."

"Ya, is tough, but okay for five dollars a day. Shoot Bird is good to me, he give me the chance of learning to drive a truck."

"You should start a business like this."

"No, I am no good sitting in a shop."

"I heard Chai is earning ten times more than you doing bully job for Yeow. Is that right?"

"I wouldn't know. I don't like to interfere with their business. They very give face to me, so I give face back to them. That's all."

Big Mole is sad to see how Kwang is changing, but feels that he is gaining inner strength in the same way his body is growing stronger.

"Chinese New Year is coming soon. By then Sachee and me will have a nicer place to stay. . . . Come and celebrate with us."

"Okay, lah, I see how first." Kwang stand up to go. "Another time!"

"Stay longer for coffee when you do. Sachee miss you!"

Big Mole watches Kwang bike away in pants instead of shorts, a young man whose spark has died with the uncertainty of what the future brings between himself and Kim.

Time flies and things change. Shoot Bird dies suddenly of a heart attack and the Spider Olympic Games die with him. Playing with wrestling spiders is no longer so exciting. Everywhere throughout Singapore people are calling for independence against the British. Strikes hit hard at the deep-water harbor of the rubber factories and the ports. Many leaders are in jail. The whole nation is in an uproar. Supporters of the strikes say, "We must eat the white man raw!"

Kwang has lost his job and is becoming desperate. Yeow, who sees his desperation, lends him money freely.

"Just use it first," he smile until proud Kwang feels shy to take it anymore.

And then Yeow says with a false tongue, "Why not go and see Big Mole? You say she is doing well. She should be able to fit you in. She probably would welcome a hand from you."

"She has already ask me to join her," Kwang admit.

"So what's the worry? Why don't you accept?"

"It is her hard-earned rice bowl. The place is too small for three. . . . There's just enough for her and Sachee to slot in."

"I suppose you are right. . . . What about all those other spider guys who give face to you all over the place? At least some of them should be able to score something better for you?"

"What can they do? They are all trapped, with no proper jobs."

"If that is the case, how do they find their eats?" Yeow grin wolfishly. "I can't understand. Surely they must have some loopholes?"

"Most of them are into stealing for the thieves' market in Sungei Road. . . . Some are eating lame ducks, robbing taxi drivers, couples at night around the Jalan Bersah Stadium, the water reservoirs, those kind of places. They have asked me to join them but I can't do it. It's just not for me, that kind of stuff."

"Ya, there is no dignity in it. . . ."

"Crawling like worms to hit the weak for shits, I rather rob the bank or kidnap the rich if I have the contacts."

"You are right. This is a black-eat-black world. There's no justice."

"I know."

"Sometimes we just have to close one eye to get somewhere?"

"True."

"With you and me together . . . We should be able to team up on something with more fats to see the daylight ahead."

Kwang knows that Yeow don't say something for nothing. "I am jam," he grin. "If you have any contact . . . draw it out, lah!"

"The picture is rather complicated," Yeow begin with pretend reluctance. And then cunning, "I can't go further with an empty belly. I'm hungry, let's go for a feed together before we have a proper talk. Satay okay?"

Penniless Kwang was hungry at the sound of good food and simply can't refuse the double temptation. They catch a trishaw to Elizabeth Walk and Yeow asks to check Kwang's feelings, "Have you seen Kim lately? I have not noticed you and her together for quite a while."

"I am getting fed up with her. . . . She is changing."

"What about her and Big Mole? Are they still together? I have lost touch with them."

"Ya, now and again."

"And that little monkey, Sachee?"

"Doing better than me. He is happy like crazy when two of his fighting fish came out with a few hundred babies recently."

"Aha! No wonder he sneak round to get some of my smaller boys to work for him."

"Ya? For what?"

"Catch red water fleas in their filthy drains for feed his baby fishes, I suppose."

"You mind?"

"No, not at all," Yeow admit. "He makes me laugh, that's all. I wish he could take away all those little mouths from me, all they do is eat, eat, eat. Frankly I wouldn't know where to chuck them away."

After their satay meal they relax on a seaside bench and smoke.

"Let me go back to the same point on the picture we mention

before," Yeow says. "It will make us rich. I believe you are still interested?"

"Talk it out, lah."

"Just between you and me first, right?"

"I give you my word."

"You must have a fair idea about Chap Jee Kee."

"Everybody knows about it."

"But do you know how much money those faceless bastards on the top make . . . ?" Yeow stares at Kwang.

Kwang did not blink.

"They eat people up without a drop of blood on the floor, right? Fat like hell. Those bastards are the worst cutthroats, been cheating people for far too long.

"Have you ever wondered how they operate it, how they laugh away with enough fats to buy the banks?"

"They pay a lot of hands and legs to shadow for them, that's all."

"Exactly! I am glad we are hitting somewhere." Yeow is excited but he quickly cool down. "If they can get their hands and legs to shadow them, why can't we? You have enough spider mates in every corner to do the same thing. I know they are invisible, but . . . who can say we can't compete with them? Guess it yourself!"

The idea hits the very center of Kwang's shark head. "You mind to pass me a smoke?" he ask to play for time.

Yeow hand him a cigarette and light it for him. "You know what I mean, then?"

"Ya, many of my old spider mates will do anything for something that big. They are not scared of anybody, only scared of the police. The police have guns."

"Don't worry about the cops, lah. Gambling is not a big offense. If they get caught, I bail them out. Same as the Chap Jee Kee runners, that's how they operate."

"If you are serious, I think my mates will listen to me. Any idea what is the cut for the show?"

"Depends."

"Why?"

"Nobody is equal, some longer, some shorter. . . . Same as fingers on the hands. If they are better, we pay more."

Kwang grin. "What about me, for example?"

Yeow smile back. "You jack up the crew, I front up the cash. Make it equal between us. Fair?"

"Have you talked to Chai about it yet?"

"No, Chai's head is too thick. Unless we agree first."

"I have to discuss with some of my mates, let you know."

"Sure, but before we go back I think it is better for us to come up with something solid together first."

"When?"

"Now, if you like. The plan has been incubating in my head for a long time. . . . Might as well draw it on the sand in front of us to clear it out!" Yeow smile.

"Might as well, lah," Kwang grin. And they jump over the concrete fence of Elizabeth Walk to reach the sand.

Yeow who was born on a grassy grave when his mother go into labor while passing the cemetery has the ability to grasp detail exactly. "As you know"—he draw a circle with a glance up at Kwang—"Singapore is divided into fifty-two districts. In every district you know the chief of the spider boys, right?"

"Right."

"Good. . . . And every chief knows their own territory inside out. Correct?"

"Go on."

"Can they recruit at least a dozen good hands who are willing to work quietly for them?"

"Easy like hell."

"From what I heard, each Chap Jee Kee runner can collect at least two to five hundred from the punters. This is only a low guess." Yeow writes down the figures.

"Let's say we have fifty-two districts times twelve runners, equals six hundred twenty-four times only two hundred dollars: That comes to one hundred twenty-four thousand eight hundred dollars each day. From what I heard, those bastards distribute only half of the collected cash back. But not us. We throw back seventy percent to keep our punters happier and still have enough left to pay everyone. We should be able to divide ten percent between us."

"Five is enough for me!"

"That means you're in?"

Kwang jokes, "Seventy percent already!"

"Well, if that's the case, let's split now. You find out more from your mates. Then we talk again. Okay? But before you go back for your bicycle, I think you should have some of this first."

Yeow pulls out his purse with a few hundred in big notes to cuff it on Kwang's hand.

"This is just oil money from both of us in advance. Even if they all say no, I am happy to forget it."

In the taxi on the way back, Yeow feels he has finally caught Kwang. Just before they go their different directions, Yeow smile and say, "A leader is a good judge who can pick the right horses to be first past the winning post."

Kwang just grins and says nothing. He likes the new Chap Jee Kee idea, but not the way Yeow dominates him with questions all the way, like a boss.

Just as a spark can create a fire, Kwang feel uncomfortable about Yeow's ways. To play safe he decides to find out exactly where Yeow is living, something he has never bothered to do before.

Chapter Eighteen

SITTING
ON A
ROCK

Kwang spend the next few days looking for his chosen spider boys. All of them were happy when they heard about the Chap Jee Kee idea and agree to discuss it together as a team. Redhill was chosen as the best place for the meeting, mainly because it was memorable to each of them, especially now Kwang was leading them to a new destiny that was fat and rewarding. They were lost without a real leader they can respect to guide them. Even the adults within their territories were getting scared at them sprouting up as the toughest youth gang and because they have no hang-ups about fear at such an age.

It was a great social occasion when they met again together in one place. Their meeting was brief and straightforward. After Kwang has explained the facts and figures in drawings on the red earth he said, "No matter what happens, we must stand together through thick and thin!"

"For sure! For sure!" everybody nods with approval.

But the hotheaded ones say, "If anyone dares to be funny with us, we melt them down!"

"That's for sure . . . !" reply the hungry ones. "We have nothing to be afraid of, nothing more to lose!"

"Who is the backer?" the smart ones ask Kwang when he stand up from squatting down among them.

"I promise not to mention his name," Kwang said straight, though he had two minds about Yeow.

"Why he hide his face on the same cake and put you in the open?" the smart ones warn. "Don't let him fool you!"

"Ya . . . ! Ya . . . !" the rest start to say. "Don't let him fool you . . . ! He sounds like a double-headed snake! Check his head and tail first!"

"I know, I know," Kwang reply thoughtfully. "I will make sure I dig him inside out. I wouldn't let you all lose face."

After more talk they agree to wait for confirmation.

The next day Kwang went to look for Chai who is making side money as a loan shark. In Chinatown, below the flat hilltop on Santeng, he found him busy polishing his new motorbike.

"Chai . . . !" Kwang playfully jab his big arm from behind.

The jab was solid and it hurts a bit. Chai jerks around with a bull-dog frown to see who.

Kwang grin. "Have you seen Yeow anywhere?"

"No," Chai slip his tongue easily with Kwang. "He must be in his nest at Katong with some girls."

"Katong? Where . . . ?"

"Neat place! Twenty-one Seaview Road. But don't disturb him! He want to be quiet about his women, keep this between you and me."

"Don't worry," Kwang reply. "Just curious. I wait for next time I see him."

Yeow has phoned Cheong Pak to come to Katong, talk about the feasibility of the Chap Jee Kee idea. After two cups of coffee Cheong Pak finally agree, but warn with finger in the air, "Regardless, you must plan an escape route for yourself. The old snakes behind Chap Jee Kee will try to hang you. They'll know exactly what to do, they will avoid Kwang's young claws in every district. They don't want to see blood on the floor, it will disrupt established business. They'll use the police to pick them up."

"Don't worry about me." Yeow light up a Lucky Strike and smile. "I have worked that out. Kwang has promised silence for me. . . . I know how to play shadow boxing with those old snakes."

"A name . . . tell me your organization's name. A name must come first."

"Chap Jee Kee run under the name Old Company. Turn it around a bit . . . call it New Company."

"Perfect!" Cheong Pak exclaim, quietly proud. "I'm looking forward to seeing what Kwang can come up with now."

* * *

Kwang has the ability to turn over every leaf from the way he hunt the evasive wrestling spiders for years. That afternoon he caught up with Yeow at his favorite coffee shop by the picture comic stall.

"Hey . . . !" Yeow look up and smiles at the sight of him. "You come at the right time. . . . I was about to look for you."

"Ya?"

"Ya, let's walk away from here."

On the slopes of Santeng, Yeow ask, "How is luck with your spider guys?"

"They are all keen. I come back early to let you know." Kwang grin. "Where are you staying now?"

"Pasir Panjang," Yeow lie without hesitation. "Why?"

"Save time looking for you. Why stay so far?"

"Good for fishing. I caught a big one the other day. You like fishing?"

"Now and again." Kwang dig further. "What is your house number?"

"Forty-three, opposite Haw Par Villa," Yeow give Ng Koo's address. "My funny landlord doesn't like visitors. . . . I only rent a room there."

"Can I phone you, just in case?"

"No phone yet, that's the only problem," Yeow curse. "By the way . . . what did your guys say about our deal?"

"They are all for it. But they want to see some money on the table first. I can't answer them. It is up to you."

"I have to work that out. . . . I am prepared to front up a week's wages in advance for them to try things out, see how it goes. By the way, how many guys do you think you can round up? I mean, all together?"

"Hard for me to say, depends on how much you want to spend."

"Let's say one chief, one deputy, and ten legs in each district," Yeow works out the numbers writing on his palm. "Na, fifty-two times twelve equals six hundred twenty-four times roughly fifty dollars a week each, equals thirty-one thousand two hundred dollars."

"Wheeoou!" Kwang whistle at the figure.

"Should be more, if everything is smooth." Yeow smile. "You will be fat . . . driving a car!"

"It is a very big gamble for you."

"Life is a gamble," Yeow smile. "I will be ready when you are, okay?"

"Say a few days' time?"

"No problem," he pats Kwang's back. "I can wait."

But Kwang feels the pat as a further insult to his pride and decides to bike straight away to Katong to find out if Chai is right.

Kwang leaves his bike a few doors away from 21 Seaview Road in case Yeow returns ahead of him by taxi. But when he saw the tidy bungalow fenced by thick shrubs with all the windows closed he knew there was nobody inside and made a quick leap over the gate for a proper look around. He recognizes Yeow's shoes outside the front door. "If you don't trust me, how can I trust you," he thinks and decides to find out the whole truth behind the smiling wolf.

He knows he has to get inside the house for more clues. From Katong he bikes to a boarding house in Joo Chiat, a middle-class area not far away, looking for an ex-spider boy who has become a burglar, to borrow a skeleton key.

The burglar has just woken from a midnight job. Inside his room there is no table and no chairs, just a bed and a basin to wash his face.

"Hey, Hong!" Kwang sit on his bed. "Talk give face. Can you lend me a wire?"

The burglar is light and small. He hands Kwang a skeleton key and ask, "What's the loopholes?"

"Nothing much. Looking for a snake. . . ."

"Kidnapping, or personal?"

"Na, personal. When do you want it back?"

"No hurry, up to you," and they talk about old times.

The next morning in Katong, Kwang sees that some of the windows of Yeow's house are open. He waits behind a tree for almost three hours before his patience runs out. Then his eyes almost drop out of his head! Kim and Yeow, holding hands, come out of the tidy bungalow.

Everything inside Kwang was sinking. He lost his will to follow them and just watched them disappear toward the main road.

Using his skeleton key, he walks inside the bungalow. In the bedroom he can smell Kim's smells on the bed, he can even recognize a few of her long black hairs left on the sheets. He feels sick and walks out through the back door leading to the beach.

He sits on a rock with his mind fighting against his broken heart. "You have no right over Kim! You lost her long ago to your spiders!" But man-to-man with Yeow he feels cheated like mad and begin to wonder why he mention the house in the superrich area of Pasir Panjang.

After Yeow drop Kim off at Ho Swee Hill he phone powerful Ng Koo, planning to use her contacts to attack the old Chap Jee Kee establishment if necessary.

By the time Yeow arrive, Ng Koo has showered after tennis and is in a silky gown with fresh makeup. She sits on her bed and says to Yeow, "I thought you were going to forget me!"

"How can I?" Yeow buries his face in her big perfumed breasts.

"Where have you been for the last two weeks, hmmm?"

Yeow lift his face up sadly and bluff. "Trouble with my godfather's business . . . he is not happy with me. I have been organizing a little business for myself."

Ng Koo kisses him and asks, "Are you worried about money?"

"No, not so much . . . more the gangs and the cops . . . too much trouble. They want too much protection money."

"Why don't you close it down?"

"To close down is to lose face. . . . Where am I going to hide my face?

"Anyway, it is not your problem, forget it! I should not let it spoil our fun now. It's my fault. . . ." He pulls a long face and lights a cigarette. And blows out smoke rings with his head resting between her legs.

Ng Koo cannot bear her pet's sad look. She steals his cigarette to smoke herself and says, "Don't worry. I can help you. Let me know who they are! I will get them for you. . . . They are only small flies in my eyes."

"That will be my last resort. . . . I'll do my best not to bother you." Yeow is the great pretender, leaving a fine gap open for Chap Jee Kee. And then he makes love to her hard and often, although tired from the whole night with Kim who he really loves.

Meanwhile Kwang is still dreaming in his new lonely world on his seaside rock in Katong. Nothing lasts forever. The tide has reached its peak. The dust inside his head has settled. A sudden wave splashes its tail to wet his pants.

On his way back through Geylang he visit Big Mole and Sachee. Big Mole was counting her day's takings on the counter with the shop about to close.

"Hey . . . Big Mole! Where is Sachee?"

"Behind the shop," Big Mole says sadly. "He won't listen to me. . . . I am so worried about him . . . !"

"What's wrong with him?" Kwang ask.

"He says he is going to kill Chai . . . ," she chokes.

"Tell me what happen. . . ." Kwang lean over the counter and take her in his arms.

"You go and look at his face first." She wipes her wet eyes with the back of her hand and goes away to close the shop.

Behind the shop which is divided by a curtain there are half a dozen big dragon pots used for preserving eggs where Sachee keeps his baby fighting fishes. As Kwang came in he saw Sachee sharpening a slim fruit knife on the lip of a dragon pot.

"Sachee," Kwang call out. "What happen to you?"

Sachee look up with one eye closed. Half of his face is swell up like pig face.

"I don't want to talk," he shouts with mouth crooked to one side.

"When is this happen?" Kwang knew it was Chai's job straightaway.

"I don't want to talk!"

"Don't be stupid! Look after your face first!"

"What do you expect me to do?" Sachee strikes downward with his knife.

"Do you want to make Big Mole cry?"

Sachee slash with the knife again. "Do you expect me to sit down and cry?"

At that moment Big Mole walk in. She look at Sachee and shout, "You better see a doctor!"

"Don't be so stupid." Kwang caught Sachee's wrist gently and took away the knife. "Listen to me, give face to Big Mole, see the doctor first, come on."

Sachee nods slightly and walks ahead stompily with his head down. Fuming about Chai who smash his face with one punch, when he attack the big bully slapping one of his recruits who catch water fleas for baby fighting fish.

The doctor, an old Malay with a gray beard, is also the local headman inside the kampong where Big Mole and Sachee live. He practice his trade in a tidy house surrounded by a few coconut trees. After looking at Sachee he laid him on a sliding chair. He cover Sachee's face with wet herbs and ask Big Mole, "What is his name?"

"His name is Sachee. We grow up together."

"Hmm, I see. Yourself?"

"My name is Big Mole." She point under her mole.

"I mean your real name."

"I don't know, tuan," Big Mole shakes her head miserably. "I don't know who is my Mama and Papa, tuan."

The doctor ponder awhile and says, "Let me take a look at your mole." He gently lifts up her chin to press a fingertip around the mole.

"Something wrong?" Big Mole ask nervously.

"No, no," he smile. "Would you like me to remove this for you?"

"Ya . . . ! Can you?" Big Mole look quietly up at him, like she looking at a god. Her eyes were shining nervously.

"Yes, it is not hard to take it out. There will be no scars in a few months after the operation." The doctor is like a loving grandfather. "Do you want me to do it?"

"Painful?" Sachee interrupt from his sliding chair.

"Less painful than yours," the doctor smile at him and to reassure Big Mole.

"I . . . I am not sure I have enough money to pay you, tuan." Big Mole bite her fingernail.

"Give me some fish when I come to your shop. I will give them to my grandchildren."

Big Mole cry with joy. "When can I do it?"

"Come and see me when you feel ready."

"Then I will wait for Sachee's face to get well first."

The old man nods contentedly and looks at Sachee. The small boy's face was numbed with potent herbs. The doctor removes them and draws out some blood with a needle to reduce the swelling. Sachee was given some ointment to use at home and a further appointment to see him in three days' time.

On their way to Big Mole's house, Kwang told them about Kim and Yeow. Big Mole advise him to stay away from Yeow without mentioning anything about Kim.

Sachee was still grumbling about Chai. Kwang also feels Chai is too much for beating up a small boy.

"Sachee," he said. "Make sure your face is okay first. I will do something on Chai for you when I am ready."

Once Sachee knew that Kwang is behind him, he feel a lot better and said, "Big Brother, stay with us...! I will do anything for you!"

"Ya," said Big Mole. "Why don't you stay with us tonight. Go back tomorrow."

After a heartbreak day, Kwang agree.

Their two-bedroom house under new atap roof has proper wallpaper. Each room has a raised plank floor and mosquito nets under straw mats. There is a reasonable-size lounge where they sit around a square table to eat Malay curry from nearby stalls.

Later that night all three of them were having mixed thoughts. Sachee in his own room was sleep-talking about Chai. Big Mole in hers was looking forward to having her mole removed and can't sleep. Kwang was thinking about Yeow and Kim on a spare canvas bed in the lounge. As his thoughts drift, he begins to wonder again why Yeow mentions the place in Pasir Panjang.

Yeow was thinking about his new Chap Jee Kee enterprise. His head was under Ng Koo's arm, cushioned against her blousy chest. She was sound asleep with her leg thrown across his naked body.

Chai was sleeping in the brothel with his favorite whore in Keong Saik Road in the outer part of Chinatown.

Cheong Pak also has a restless night in Neil Road on the edge of Chinatown. He stops reading his newspaper under a table lamp by the bedside and say, "Hey, Cigarette Woman! You think I should pay old Wong a visit in Ho Swee Hill?"

"What is on your mind, Old Fox?" she reply on the bed, stitching on a missing button on Yeow's shirt.

"There is a chance he still has some clues regarding Chap Jee Kee. He was the one who started it all."

"I doubt it." She bite away the cotton on the button.

"The potential is there, anyway. I am sure he wouldn't mind me paying him a visit."

"If you are going, remember to bring him some old mud, that might be handy. Have you talked to Yeow?"

"No, I don't want to complicate things for him."

"How soon?"

"I will give Yeow and Kwang a week to settle first."

"I'll leave it all to you, then." She stand up to roll a cigarette to smoke before going to bed.

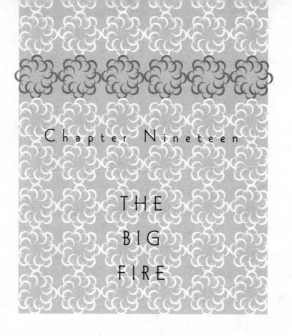

Chapter Nineteen

THE
BIG
FIRE

The next morning Kwang bikes straight from Big Mole's shop to Pasir Panjang with its large expensive houses perched on a thirty-meter cliff looking out to sea. The tar-sealed road running past them was empty of traffic and lined with tall bushy trees. High walls studded with broken glass protected the houses from the street. After biking for two hours from the opposite end of Singapore, Kwang found only a postman riding a bike ahead of him. The postman whistled as he stopped at number 43 and pressed the bell by a gate with barbed wire on top. A hunched back old gatekeeper reached out through the iron bars to take the letters.

Through the gate Kwang could see only a red sports car with a canvas hood on the big parking area so he climbed a tree outside the wall to scout inside. His heart jumps at the site of Yeow sunbathing with a topless woman under a black-and-white umbrella by the swimming pool. Her big tits swung lazily as she massaged sun lotion on Yeow's back. Yeow was sucking from a green coconut through a straw.

So Yeow had a tiger woman backing him! That was how he could come up so easily with thousands of dollars in advance! Kwang grinned as he climbed down the tree. He has had enough of Yeow's lying and bikes away to see Hong, the burglar in the boarding house at Joo Chiat.

A gentle knock on the door is enough to wake him.

"Who is that?" the burglar answers sleepily.

"Hong . . . ! Is me, Kwang!"

"Come in, come in," he yawn with arms stretched up. "How is everything, smooth?"

"Wash your face first." Kwang close the door.

"How was my wire?" Hong ask as he brush his teeth.

"Not rusty," Kwang refer to the skeleton key he uses at Katong.

"So?" Hong giggle with his mouth full of fresh water.

"Can you give face one more time?"

"Friendship is for free. Any time for you. Why?"

"There is another house with walls like Changi prison."

"Na, every house has a hole," Hong dismiss the problem. "You need a hand?"

*　　*　　*

On their way to catch a taxi back to Pasir Panjang, Kwang mention the Chap Jee Kee scheme and his reason for wanting to get back at Yeow. The burglar remembers Kim with Kwang at the Spider Olympics.

"I understand how you feel. I used to have a girlfriend too. How are you going to hit back at the double-headed snake?"

"Take his Chap Jee Kee money first, sort him out later. Something like that."

They stop the taxi a few doors away from Ng Koo's mansion. The burglar, who is five foot two, look up at the wall and says, "That is easy, only fourteen feet!"

"Feel like checking inside tonight?"

"Na, save that for later. See who or what is backing him first. Otherwise keep cool."

"My mates still don't know that Yeow is behind the Chap Jee Kee scheme, they will lose face if I tell them exactly what has happened, think I have wasted everything because of a girl. I don't want to be called names behind my back."

"Na, why worry? Play straight is better . . . lose a bit of face is nothing. If they are your real friends they will understand . . . !"

"You think we should go and see some of them now?"

"Why not," reply Hong, who play with spiders long before Kwang. "Might as well borrow a few hands to count the snakes behind that big wall."

On the other side of the busy main road, bushy land is divided into many muddy tracks, the main one leads into the slum village part of Pasir Panjang where many retired spider boys live in small gangs. Inside their atap houses Kwang told the truth only to his top spider boy. Although younger than them, Kwang is still their hero.

"So what if his name is Chinatown Yeow?" the spider boy swear. "Leave him to me!"

"No, no," the burglar wave a cautious finger. "One step at a time. Pick a few of your hands to watch the place. If we are going to chop the grass, make sure we get out the roots!"

After two days of careful watching and taking down the numbers of the cars of Ng Koo's clients, Hong asks the spider boys, "Did any of them return the next day?"

"No, but the red car owned by the woman is always there."

"What about the young girls that came by taxi?"

"Can't see their faces at night. But they left in big cars with the old European and Chinese."

"That means the place is also a whorehouse," Hong said to the younger boys watching for him. "That's good enough. Tonight I will go inside when everyone is snoring like pigs, check the layout but move out with nothing."

"Ya," Kwang nods, "once I get the money from his hands we'll move in with our guys for another trick."

Kwang decided to visit the pet fish shop in Geylang with Hong and told him the story of Sachee on the way.

"Poor kid," Hong shakes his head. "I can't stand bullies."

"You should meet Big Mole too. Nice girl, solid inside."

"Good-looking?"

"Na, not very."

"What is looks? You fancy her?"

"Just good friends."

Sachee with a net in one hand was suggesting some fish to younger customers and didn't see them come in. Hong gaze round with hand on sharp chin and nods at Kwang, "Good spot, well set up."

"Is hard work, long hours," Big Mole smile at him.

"At least you are your own boss," Hong comment, looking at Sachee whose face is still badly bruised.

"Do you want a coffee or are you in a hurry? The coffee stall is just around the corner."

Sachee had finally convinced his clients to buy a few stripey angel fish and was delighted to meet Hong who knows quite a lot about fighting fish. Hong suggest to Sachee about using dry banana leaves inside the dragon pots. "Give them a chance to hide when they fight. Also helps to make the water cooler."

When Kwang came back with coffee in used milk cans with grass straws attached their conversation became more general as they discovered common ground. Although Hong never mentions his profession, they all have a fair idea of the meaning of the differences between the rich and very poor.

After Kwang picked up his bike at Hong's place he went straight to his appointment with Yeow on top of Santeng. Chai was with Yeow when he arrived, carrying the Chap Jee Kee cash in a shoulder bag.

"Is all here," Yeow pats Chai's bag and flashes his famous smile. "I have talked to Chai about it. I hope you don't mind."

"Don't worry about it," Kwang grin. "I expect Chai to know sooner or later."

"How is everything on your side?"

"Everybody is willing to die for it."

"I have counted the money twice," Yeow smile at him. "Do you want to double-check it for yourself?"

Kwang avoids Yeow's eye and turns aside to peer inside Chai's shoulder bag and joke, "As long as it is not cardboard. We are talking trust now, aren't we?"

"No worries," Yeow reply. "Why not leave it just like that?"

Kwang takes the bag and hangs it over his shoulder, remembering what Hong say and careful not to talk too much more.

"Just before you go . . . ," said Yeow, "I think Chai should come along and meet your crew."

"Tonight?"

"Ya, that is why he is here. I should have mention it earlier."

"Tonight we are getting together because of this," Kwang pats his bag of money. "I don't know how to explain to them if Chai comes along without warning. Make it Sunday, for a proper introduction? I have to give face to them too."

Yeow look at Chai, who don't like to offend Kwang who he has fought with so many times.

"Is the same thing, Yeow. Sooner or later I will meet them. . . ."

Yeow was looking to the future and didn't want to make a fuss about present money. He finally agrees against his instincts and lets Kwang slip away to get more advice from Hong.

From Santeng, Yeow went back to Cigarette Woman's place to see Cheong Pak but his godfather was not there.

"I should not hide anything from you. Cheong Pak went to see

Wong inside Ho Swee Hill, to talk about the old days in Hon Moon."

Cheong Pak, who smoke opium himself, has bought some extra as a present for Wong who was brushing works on red paper when the surprise visitor knock at his door.

"Can I come in?" Cheong Pak bow slightly in his conservative Chinaman's clothing. Wong threw down his brush at the sight of his old-time comrade.

"Please sit down! Please sit down!" he grin from tobacco-colored teeth.

"I hope I am not disturbing you?" Cheong Pak sit cross-legged on the settee.

"Not at all. What a rare occasion!"

Wong serve his visitor hot coffee from a vacuum flask and ask, "What winds blow you here after all these years?"

"I must admit, I come to seek your advice."

"What is the storm about?"

"It is not easy to put it in a few words." Cheong Pak pulls his opium from his sleeve. "I need some of this old habit to light up my thoughts with you. I hope you will accept this bit of meaning?" He passes over the opium using two hands in the old-fashioned way.

Wong took the opium and said, "I have lost touch with the outside world. How are you?"

"Still living on newspapers in Santeng."

"And your wife?"

"Selling bits of cigarette. Yours?"

"A seamstress now. Has just gone out to deliver some clothing."

"Any future seeds?"

"His name is San, born during the Japanese occupation. Yourself?"

"No more since my son change body. To recover from his death, my wife adopted another son, a young man restless as the wind."

"Winds don't allow trees to grow in peace. So how is he?"

"I won't hide from you. He is not making a straight living. My wife is worried."

"What is he up to?"

"Trying to set up his own Chap Jee Kee operation."

"That is a real problem. Someone will hang him for it."

"Can you prevent it?"

"No, he has to stop by himself."

"I can't help him . . . and there is more than that. He is working with some of the young ones inside this village."

"Do you know their names?" Wong asks with sudden concern.

Cheong Pak takes the opportunity to mention Kwang, who he knows will get some Chap Jee Kee secrets out of Wong. This leads them to smoke opium together behind the Kuan Yin Temple. They smoke and smoke and talk and talk until Wong finally says, "I will do my best for Yeow and Kwang. I owe Kwang's dead father my life." Cheong Pak is not used to smoking so much opium. When he leaves the village he nearly stumbles in the river, thinking that the water is the land.

On the same night as the moon is sinking into the sea at Pasir Panjang, Kwang and Hong were climbing up a soft ladder hooked over Ng Koo's high wall. The sharp glass set into the top of the wall was cushioned with a jute sack packed inside with sand, like a horse saddle. Once inside they explore the whole house from top to bottom and the grounds outside, from the tennis court to the swimming pool close to the edge of the cliff. Kwang points out the drop to Hong.

"When the time comes I am going to make Yeow jump from here."

The next afternoon they hire a car to distribute Yeow's money. It takes two days' cruising to cover the island country of Singapore, from the Johore Causeway to Jurong, with its mangrove swamps and rich farmland.

"If we had enough money we could buy a few kelong out there." Hong points toward the sea where there are many kelong on long stilts for fish trapping, with atap huts on top for the fishermen to live and work.

"How are you going to get the money?" Kwang asks.

"Either start our own Chap Jee Kee, or take over Yeow's territory in Chinatown. He has had it good for too long. Sachee says his boys would rather stick to you than him. They are all waiting for you to snap your fingers. . . . They must really hate Yeow and Chai to say that." Hong makes his point slowly and very clearly.

"What about Yeow?"

"You really want him to jump off the cliff?"

"Ya."

"We still need his money. Frankly, I think we should let the Chap Jee Kee run under him for a while first, see how it goes, then take him. . . ."

"You know these things better than me," Kwang admit. "I leave it to you to say when."

*　*　*

On Big Mole's day off, Sachee was looking after the shop with some of his canal boys helping. They were all talking about revenge on Chai, fanning the fire with hands eager to help.

"I am going to stab him myself," proud Sachee says. "I am still thinking how to do it properly."

"Get him when he comes out of the cinema at Nam Tain," one of the older boys suggests. "He bully one of us to buy a ticket for him, the four o'clock session which finish at six-thirty."

"Ya," another boy interrupt. "Roll a knife inside a newspaper, then stick him quickly, walk away in the crowd. No blood on hand, the police can't catch you."

Fired-up Sachee smash one hand in excited punch against the other. "Just wait and see," the small boy says.

When the movie finished Chai and a bar girl came out of the south side of the theater where Sachee was waiting behind the door. He followed them quietly and when the right time came stabbed Chai through the waist with his fruit knife that he had specially sharpened. The knife went in so quickly that Chai walked a few more steps before he felt anything, then crouched down with his hand on the handle of the knife before dropping to the ground in the middle of a suddenly screaming crowd. News travels so fast in Chinatown that it has already reached Santeng by the time Chai was in the emergency ward.

Sachee was delighted at his success and returned to Geylang to boast of it in front of Kwang and Hong, having a late-night snack with Big Mole. Big Mole had a fresh scar where her mole had been, covered in herbal oil. She was speechless at Sachee's news of what he had done but Hong pulled Kwang aside and said, "We have to change our plans, must go and get Yeow tonight instead."

* * *

Cheong Pak was unable to contact Yeow at Katong Beach because he was still sweating in bed with Ng Koo in Pasir Panjang. He immediately went to see Wong, to contact Chai's father. Wong was not at home, but at the opium den in the atap cottage behind the Kuan Yin Temple, fenced by high bamboo hedges.

Dopey Wong was at the peak of the opium's soporific effect, the place where one no longer dreams, one is the dream itself. He simply said to Cheong Pak, "That is fate. Be calm against the wave. You should check Chai's condition first."

But Cheong Pak was thinking more of Yeow.

"All I want to know is that Yeow will not act recklessly. He will suspect that Kwang is behind it all. . . . I can't afford to see a war between a tiger and a dragon."

At the same time Kwang, Hong, and five other top spider boys had already climbed inside Ng Koo's mansion. Two of the masked spider boys tied up the gatekeeper and went upstairs to join the others who had cut the telephone line. They switched on the light in the bedroom and threw a blanket over Yeow and Ng Koo's naked bodies. No one said a word. Hong opened all the drawers with his skeleton key and took out Ng Koo's diary with the names of clients inside.

"What is this?" he broke the silence. He could only read a bit of English.

Ng Koo was too shocked for words. But Yeow's nerve was still intact.

"Why don't you all just say exactly what you want?"

Hong snapped his fingers. "Money," he said. "As much as possible. Where are the keys to the safe?"

Ng Koo pointed to the drawer at the head of her large bed. Hong took out the key without a word and handed to a spider boy. All the money and the jewelry in the safe was loaded into a sack. When they returned to Ng Koo's room, Hong snapped his fingers again and said, "Now is the time for you all to have a dip in the swimming pool and watch the sunrise!"

"Do you have to tie our hands for that?" Yeow asked.

"One hand and one leg, so you walk nicely together," Hong replied.

At the edge of the pool Ng Koo was roped under the steps with her head just above the water. Then Kwang took off his mask and grinned at shocked Yeow.

"Why aren't you sleeping with Kim instead of her?"

Yeow was lost for words but then answered, "Why don't you just pull a knife through my throat if you are that jealous!"

"Because I made a promise to see you jump off a cliff instead."

Hong threw Yeow his shirt and pants. "You better put something on then before you get cold feet," Kwang said.

Below the cliff the tide was full. Yeow realized that they were going to push him over so took his time putting on his trousers. When they thought he was going to slip into his shirt he ran instead to the edge of the cliff and dived out as far as he could to avoid the rocks below, using the moonlight reflected from the water as his guide.

At such a deadly moment the mind speeds faster than the imagination to make time stand still. The only person he saw at this time was Kim, one month pregnant with his baby.

He crashed down through the waves and began to swim for shore. When he finally reached the beach he set out at once to find her at Ho Swee Hill.

Coincidence sometimes happens like in a fairy tale. Wong was in an emotional state, still smoking opium and thinking about Kwang's long-dead father who arrived in Singapore from China on the junk *Nam Hong* at Amoy. The opium den was bare and lonely without all the old vibrations. It was dark and damp and the small kerosene lamp was running out of fuel. Wong added more kerosene and mumbled, "Tonight I am going to smoke my way to heaven!" And sucked his opium pipe to finish a standard spot of opium on one go.

The effect on the calligrapher was ecstatic. His head went *zong zong zong*, everything was imagery. "I am proud to face heaven!" he shouts inside his head. "I have done nothing wrong! Pau Shen! Pau Shen! Where are you?"

Kwang's father appears before him with a few acrobatic flips. "It is me!" He folds his arms with a steel-tight grin. "Four Eyes! Big Head is worse than you!" They are nicknames for Wong and for Chai's father, who all came on the same boat together with Pau Shen.

Lying on his side in a trance, Wong stretched out his legs and kicked over the kerosene lamp. The next moment he saw fire, fire on the floor spreading up the dry wooden walls and with a *whoof* bursting through the atap roof. It turned the opium den in the false ceiling into an inferno. He stumbled down the creaky ladder and out of the blazing cottage with ataps flying in the wind like cotton wool. And wakes the whole village with screams of "Fire! Fire!"

Like a zombie, Wong walks out of the burning village amidst the cries of the fleeing to No Nose Bridge, under the sky which was getting redder and redder. On the bridge he saw Ho Swee River turn red, he saw refugees running faster than during the Japanese occupation. He recognized countless of them and tried to talk to them, but no one answered back.

He felt loss, he felt rage. He stared at the red reflection in the river, like a meaningless ghost in a vacuum, so light that he could jump down and fly away to meet old mates in a more real world. "I am only one step away from heaven!" he cried. He placed one foot on the railings of the bridge, trembling under the feet of running refugees.

"Mr. Wong! Mr. Wong! What are you doing?" The familiar voice of Kwang's mother was calling to him. He saw her and Kwang's two little brother, with sarongs tied into bags over their shoulder to carry whatever possession they could. "Where are you going, Mr. Wong?" she ask again.

Wong wakes up out of the blue. He grins his tobacco teeth at her. "I come with you and give you a hand." He takes the weight from Yee's shoulder and they join the refugees out of Ho Swee Hill.

Yeow too saw the fire as he approached the village. He couldn't find Kim in the crowds of running people but he did see Kwang, searching for his little brothers. They both stood still and stared at each other for a long time.

It was Yeow who reached out his hand to shake with Kwang.

"I know how you feel. I feel the same. Are we evened out now?"

Kwang answers, "It is already even."

"We are free, then," Yeow offers. "I am not going back to Chinatown."

"Katong Beach with Kim then?" Kwang force a grin.

"Ya," says Yeow, and slowly walk away.

[ends]